CANDLELIGHT

Supreme

**"ROBERT!" MAGGIE SCREAMED, AS A
HISSING NOISE ECHOED THROUGH THE LAB.
"I'M GOING TO KILL YOU!"**

Before either of them could say another word, there was
a loud *plop,* and the facial cream Robert had been cooking up spewed from his lab equipment, raining down on
top of them.

"Maggie, I'm sorry," Robert began, as the white goo
streamed down his face. "Here, let me—"

"Don't touch me!" she cried. "You planned this, you
. . . you crazy inventor. Why won't you get out of my
life once and for all?"

"Don't be silly, I . . ." A frown furrowed his goo-
covered brow. "Oh, Lord," he moaned as he felt his forehead. "This stuff is beginning to harden."

Maggie tried to point an accusing finger at him, but
they were all stuck together. "I knew it! You've glued us
together!"

CANDLELIGHT SUPREMES

MY DARLING PRETENDER

Linda Vail

A CANDLELIGHT SUPREME

Published by
Dell Publishing Co., Inc.
1 Dag Hammarskjold Plaza
New York, New York 10017

ISBN: 0-440-15279-8

Printed in the United States of America

October 1986

10 9 8 7 6 5 4 3 2 1

WFH

To Our Readers:

We are pleased and excited by your overwhelmingly positive response to our Candlelight Supremes. Unlike all the other series, the Supremes are filled with more passion, adventure, and intrigue, and are obviously the stories you like best.

In months to come we will continue to publish books by many of your favorite authors as well as the very finest work from new authors of romantic fiction. As always, we are striving to present unique, absorbing love stories —the very best love has to offer.

Breathtaking and unforgettable, Supremes follow in the great romantic tradition you've come to expect *only* from Candlelight Romances.

Your suggestions and comments are always welcome. Please let us hear from you.

Sincerely,

The Editors
Candlelight Romances
1 Dag Hammarskjold Plaza
New York, New York 10017

CHAPTER ONE

"If this perfume doesn't drive men wild, can I get my money back?"

"Of course," Maggie Johnson assured the customer, her voice serene, just as she had been trained by the store personnel a short week ago. "Thank you for shopping with us."

Wiggling her toes discreetly, Maggie shifted from one foot to the other, feeling as if she was being tortured by her high-heeled shoes. This job was giving her a new respect for saleswomen who were on their feet all day. She would never gripe about sitting behind a desk again.

"Ms. Johnson, I'd like you to relieve Ms. English over at the pink counter," the head of the department informed her. "And please remember to color coordinate your jacket."

"Of course, Mrs. Williams," Maggie replied. Heaven forbid she wear the soft peach-colored linen jacket in an area designed for pale pink.

Finally, a chance to move around and get out from behind the perfume counter she'd been assigned to for the last three days. The constant assault of so many different scents was taking its toll on her sense of smell—and her patience. At least the creams and beauty products displayed so enticingly along the pink counter had lighter fragrances.

As a temporary worker who usually ended up typing and filing in an office, Maggie had jumped at the chance to try something so different from secretarial work. The posh surroundings of the prestigious department store in Dallas were wearing thin, however, and she was thankful this was her last night on the job.

It was just her luck that this particular Sunday evening required her to work late; she didn't know if her poor feet could take any more of this constant torture. Tomorrow she started an assignment with a company she'd worked for recently. The job would entail a lot of overtime, but at least she'd be sitting down for those extra hours, not standing.

Maggie sighed and stifled a yawn, trying not to look as bored as she felt. To keep her mind occupied she scanned the crowd of shoppers, spotting a man she had noticed wandering around the cosmetics department earlier.

"I wonder if he's trying to get up his nerve to buy something," she murmured to herself when she caught sight of him near a display for a new beauty cream.

He seemed engrossed as he read the ad promising results almost instantly. Maggie watched him for a moment, but averted her gaze when he looked up from the display.

Robert Langley, however, continued to study her quite openly. Her hair was dark brown, rich mahogany when the light hit it right, and was cut straight across her shoulders in a style that suited her beautifully. Her full lips framed a mouth he deemed definitely worth kissing. Her eyes were hazel, he noticed, expertly made-up, and she had high cheekbones, a straight nose, and lovely white teeth. Robert couldn't quite make out the details of her figure because of the long pink linen smock she wore, but she looked slender.

Smiling, he turned away and read the beauty cream ad again, chuckling at the outrageous claims. Maybe he'd ask the lovely lady behind the counter if she used this stuff. If she did, he might just become a believer.

Unable to help herself, Maggie found her eyes straying back to him. He was not the most attractive man she'd seen today, but there was something intriguing about him. Maybe it was the way his jeans hugged his strong thighs, or the way his broad shoulders encased in a red plaid shirt tapered to lean hips. Six feet or so, with dark hair worn a little longer than most, he definitely qualified as sexy in the Maggie Johnson book of desirable men.

She felt her pulse increase slightly when he turned and looked casually in her general direction. She still couldn't make out the color of his eyes, but he was clean-shaven and had a beautiful tan. He looked familiar to her but she couldn't place him. Perhaps she'd seen him on one of the many jobs she'd been on in the past few months?

Then their eyes met. His were gray. Lowering her gaze to his left hand, she noticed he wasn't wearing a wedding ring. She smiled when she saw how quickly he was crossing the aisle toward her, and Maggie promptly decided this temporary job might turn out to be interesting after all.

"Hi, I'm Robert Langley," he said, holding out his hand to her.

"Maggie Johnson," she returned, shaking his hand. He was even better close up. Yes, she thought, this job was definitely getting interesting. "May I show you something?" she asked softly.

Though he grinned and seemed about to say something else, he pointed to a cream and asked, "May I see the list of ingredients in this one, please?"

"Ingredients?" She stared at him blankly for a moment. "Oh. Certainly." Maggie handed him a large box of the cream and watched him study the contents.

"I'll take a small one of these," he said at last, handing the large box back to her. "I'd also like to see that bright red box over there." She took it from the display case and gave it to him. "Fine. I'll take this one too."

Puzzled by his businesslike tone and wondering

what he did with all these creams, Maggie managed to continue smiling politely. "Certainly, sir."

"How about the black and silver one?"

Maggie shrugged, handed the cream to him, then held up yet another box. "We have this pale yellow one as well," she told him. After all, a sale was a sale.

"No," he murmured, not looking up from his reading. "I've bought that one before."

Now her curiosity was really aroused. Who—or what—was he buying these for? She watched as he walked around the counter, a puzzled look on his face.

"Are these two by the same company?" he asked, indicating two jars with different labels behind the glass display case.

She had no idea. "Let me check."

The growing pile of beauty creams on the counter had attracted the attention of Mrs. Williams. "Can I help you?" the older woman asked Robert the moment Maggie turned her back.

"I was just getting this customer some information," Maggie interrupted briskly. Temporary position or not, this was still her sale.

"I'll take over now, Ms. Johnson. You return to perfume," she ordered.

Robert cleared his throat. "I want to deal with Maggie if you don't mind, Mrs. Williams."

"Certainly, sir." The customer was always right in this store. Her eyes shot daggers at Maggie before she left the area.

Maggie stood there, her eyebrows arched in surprise at the way this man had addressed the department head by name. She looked at him curiously, but he simply grinned.

"Nice boss you have there," Robert said dryly.

"I only work here temporarily," Maggie muttered. "Thank heavens." She handed him the two boxes. "They're made by the same company."

He read the labels and nodded. "The ingredients are almost identical too. Different perfumes probably. Are they the same color?" he asked, looking at her expectantly.

"Who knows?" She opened samples of each product and showed him the color side by side. "They look alike to me."

"Hmm. One is a bit greener. I'll take that one, and a bottle of that miracle cream on display over there."

Maggie stacked his choices on the counter beside the others. "Can I show you anything else?"

"Yes." He looked at her appraisingly, his businesslike demeanor gone.

"What would you like to see?"

"You."

"What?" She stared at him in disbelief. Just her luck this handsome stranger would turn out strange, she thought.

"Or perhaps you'd like to see me."

"Are you available?" she couldn't resist asking.

"I might be, for you."

Maggie blinked. His was the direct approach

taken one giant step into the outrageous zone. But for some reason it suited him. The indefinable attraction she'd felt for him even across the store was stronger now, too strong to ignore or walk away from.

She peered at his face, frowning. "Do I know you?" she asked.

"I'm willing."

"No, thanks," she said, having second thoughts and turning to move away. Devilish attraction or not, he was just a bit too outrageous.

"We could—"

"How would you like to pay for this?" she asked, interrupting him. Still grinning, he handed her the store credit card and watched as she busied herself filling out the charge slip and putting the various creams in a bag. "Please sign on the top line," she requested.

Robert's hand brushed hers as she pushed the slip across the counter. "Mmm. Your skin is so soft. Which of these creams do you use?" he asked, looking into her eyes.

Maggie ignored him. She only wished she could ignore the way her hand still tingled from his light touch. "Thank you for shopping with us," she said, handing him his package and turning away.

"Wait! You could at least have a drink with me. We could go somewhere quiet, maybe get to know each other better?" He noticed the way her eyebrows arched and added hastily, "Verbally."

He looked so sincere and appealing, she was definitely weakening. Maggie cocked her head to one side and looked at him, trying to figure him out. What harm could it do? After all, hadn't she decided she needed some new and unusual experiences in her life?

"I don't know. . . ."

"I'll get Mrs. Williams to vouch for me." He looked around the cosmetics area, trying to spot the department head. Clasping her hand in his, he pulled her with him.

Maggie gritted her teeth and tried to hold her ground. Not only was Mrs. Williams a rather grumpy woman to work for, she also had the reputation as a most tenacious matchmaker. Happily married for many years, she liked to see everyone else around her as blissfully wed.

Robert stopped in his tracks to avoid running into a little girl and Maggie bumped into him before she could prevent the collision. "Oops. Sorry."

"The pleasure was all mine," he replied, his dark eyebrows bobbing up and down roguishly as he turned to her, standing closer than he needed to. "Let's do it again, but facing each other this time."

Maggie chuckled in spite of the flip-flop her stomach did in reaction to his sensual innuendo. "You certainly have an inventive approach with women, Mr. Langley."

"Robert. And I have an inventive approach toward everything, Maggie," he informed her, leaning close to make himself heard over the noise of the crowded store. "Care to see for yourself?" he asked.

"Oh, Lord," she muttered. What had she gotten herself into? Mrs. Williams was coming toward them, a curious expression on her face. Maggie pulled him over to the perfume counter. "All right. But I don't get off for another fifteen minutes."

"I'll meet you back here. Will you keep track of my purchases?" he asked, setting the bag on the counter.

"Certainly."

"Then it's a date."

Maggie's pulse fluttered at the thought. She ignored the sudden uneasiness she felt and hurried to the other side of the counter to help a waiting customer, effectively cutting off Mrs. Williams's attempt to interrogate her.

While he waited, Robert wandered around the store, enjoying the tall ceilings and plush atmosphere. The whole mall had been built with money in mind, very ornate and stylish, with an open feeling he enjoyed.

He hated being hemmed in. It was a personality trait, really, a part of his philosophy of life. An inventor by trade, Robert Langley made a living—a very good living—by keeping an open mind, seeing beyond problems to the unique solutions which had given him a reputation as a creative genius. Open spaces helped him think, liberated his considerable intellect, and enabled him to concentrate on the new products or production processes that were his bread and butter.

Such a philosophy had given him another reputation as well, however. Friends and acquaintances considered him brilliant but slightly eccentric. Not an absentminded professor by any means, he did tend to ignore certain things about everyday life—wearing the same color socks, for instance, or keeping his daily logs and business files in proper order.

He was organized—a self-employed inventor had to be to survive—but his organization tended to come in fits and starts. Whenever all the nagging details started to bog him down, he simply put them aside until later. As a result, those details occasionally came cascading in on him, piling up around his feet, demanding immediate attention.

Befuddled, Robert would sort through them, make a path he could walk through, and go on to the next project until the avalanche came again. Perhaps it wasn't the most efficient way of doing things, but he managed to attain his goals nevertheless. Just saying his name over the phone got him undivided attention in most of the major southwestern manufacturing firms. Besides, in his opinion, too much organization was just another nagging detail, another fence blocking the horizon.

Back in the cosmetics department, Maggie was feeling a bit fenced in at the moment herself. Mrs. Williams was hanging around like a vulture, and Robert Langley—a stranger who seemed hung up on beauty cream—was on his way over to collect her for the insane date she'd agreed to.

Ignoring her sudden uneasiness, she punched out on the time clock, slipped on her coat, then picked up Robert's purchases and her purse. He smiled at her so winningly as he approached she almost forgot how ludicrous this whole situation was. Almost.

"What did you have in mind?" she asked as they managed to avoid Mrs. Williams and escape to the parking lot.

Robert chuckled, but replied innocently, "Coffee all right with you?"

"Fine." She sighed in relief. "I'll meet you at that all-night pancake house near the end of the street."

"You lead, I'll follow."

He waved and got into a silver Mercedes gull-wing coupe, started the engine, and pulled up behind her aging but equally German economy car. Maggie pulled away from the curb, looking at him in her rearview mirror.

"Somehow, Mr. Robert Langley," she muttered under her breath as she led the way to the coffee shop, "I get the feeling you rarely follow anybody anywhere."

"Okay, Maggie, let's set the record straight," Robert said when the waiter had taken their orders and left the table. "Are you married?"

"Are you?" she countered.

"No, never have been," he replied, holding up three fingers and grinning back at her. "Scout's honor."

"Neither have I." Though she drank it black, she picked up a spoon and absentmindedly stirred her coffee. She looked around the nearly empty café, for some reason unable to meet his devastating gray eyes for more than a few moments at a time.

"Good. Then we're free to enjoy each other."

Maggie forced herself to look at him, a perturbed expression on her face. "Robert, I—"

"Just a figure of speech," he assured her. "I don't date married, separated, or engaged women. Makes my life much simpler."

"We're not dating." As outrageous as he was, she liked him. If they could get by the awkward phase, Maggie had the distinct feeling they might be good for one another.

"But you'd like to." It wasn't a question. He smiled slightly as she stirred her coffee without adding anything.

On the other hand, this guy had an ego a mile wide. "I find it hard to believe you were ever a boy scout," she told him dryly, changing the subject.

"You're right. I wasn't."

"Drummed out of the troop?"

"No. I was too busy chasing little girls even then."

When he smiled, his whole face came alive, the lines around his smoky gray eyes deepening, adding character and depth to an already fascinating face. Maggie knew she was in trouble when he reached across the table and took her hand. She could feel his touch, not just where he stroked her but whispering through her entire body.

"I'm not a little girl," she said, the words flowing out before she could stop them.

"No, you're definitely a woman." As he caressed the palm of her hand with his thumb, his eyes caressed her as well. "And available."

She jerked her hand away, glaring at him. "I'm what?"

"Available for dating," he replied calmly. Holding his coffee mug with both hands, he looked at her over the rim. "Aren't you?"

"If I choose to be."

Taking a sip of her own coffee, Maggie grimaced in irritation. She didn't like the way this conversation was going—nor where it seemed Robert's mind was leading him. Available indeed! Self-assurance was one thing, sheer arrogance another.

Sensing her irritation, Robert asked, "Do you work full-time at the department store?"

"No," she replied, thankful for the change of subject. "It's just an assignment, one I'm happy to say is now over. I work for a temporary agency."

"Doing what?"

"All sorts of things, mainly office work."

"Hmm."

Robert watched with interest as Maggie continued to fiddle with her spoon as she talked. She had pretty hands, smooth skin, and tapered fingers; he was struck with the thought of how much he'd like to feel those hands on him, but tried to keep the sensual gleam from his eyes. She seemed skittish enough as it was.

"Until a year or so ago I was an executive secretary for a manufacturing firm here in town," she continued. "But if you don't like your boss, that kind of job can get very tiring very fast. I decided I needed a change. Rather than get back into the same old grind, I signed on with Alison Temporary Services."

"Do you like it?"

Maggie looked at him, puzzled by the intensity of his gaze. His interest appeared to be sincere, though, so she warmed to the subject. "Yes, I do. It's interesting to work in different companies, see how they operate, what they handle, and how they do it."

"How long do these jobs last?" Robert inquired in a casual tone. An intriguing idea was forming in his mind.

"It varies—anywhere from a few days to months. It depends on the job and what I want. Some companies are even looking for permanent employees, but so far I haven't found one I'd want to stay with." She looked up from her coffee and into his eyes, a frown furrowing her brow. "Why?"

He shrugged nonchalantly. "I'm just trying to get to know you, Maggie. After all," he added, grinning at her, "if we're going to be going out together—"

"Pretty sure of yourself, aren't you?" she interrupted.

Unperturbed by her accusing tone, Robert continued to smile. "Do you have another assignment lined up yet?"

"Yes. I start a new assignment tomorrow that will last all week." Maggie didn't know what to make of his sly smile. She cut him off before he could speak again and asked, "How about you, Robert? What do you do for a living?"

He averted his eyes. "I'm a blacksmith."

"Seriously."

"Don't I look like one?" he asked, feigning a sudden interest in the print hanging on the wall near their table.

"I wouldn't know," she replied dryly. "Do they have a special look about them?"

"Not really."

Maggie realized she was being teased, but it also seemed as if he was genuinely worried about telling her his true occupation. "So, are you poor? Independently wealthy? I already know you're a pain in the—"

"I'm an inventor," he inserted before she could continue.

"Of what? Stories?"

"No, things," he said, still evasive.

"Things." Maggie fixed him with a suspicious

21

gaze. "I don't suppose you'd care to be more specific?"

Robert sighed and finally returned his eyes to her face. She looked so wary he had to laugh. "Nothing sinister, I assure you. Do you watch late-night television?"

"Occasionally. What has that got to do with . . ." Her voice trailed off, her eyes opening wide in a mixture of surprise and sudden understanding. "Oh, no! You don't mean those kinds of things?"

"What's wrong with those things?" he asked, giving her a fierce look.

In her best imitation of a frantic television announcer, Maggie reeled off a list of outrageous advertising claims. "It slices, dices, minces, and chops! It'll do your laundry! It'll wash the dog and the car at the same time! Act now before our limited supply is gone. Send nineteen ninety-five and your firstborn male child to—"

"Hey!" Robert cried in a wounded tone. This was exactly why he didn't like to tell people how he got started. But he also knew that even the people who scorned those things secretly bought some of them. "I've long since moved on to bigger and better products—mainly cosmetics—but I cut my inventive teeth creating stuff like that. It paid the rent and subsidized my more serious work," he informed her in a terse, defiant tone.

Maggie couldn't stop laughing. "I'm sorry, but really! Some of those commercials," she managed to say, wrinkling her nose in distaste.

"Okay, so the companies I sold my ideas to were hardly masters of good taste," he admitted wryly, joining in her laughter. "I didn't come up with the commercials, just the products."

She liked his laugh. It was a relief to know he didn't take himself as seriously as she had first thought. So he was an inventor. No wonder he seemed a bit eccentric and had such an unusual approach to everything.

"Do people really buy those things?"

"Do you expect me to believe you've never checked your mailbox every day, anxiously awaiting the arrival of some wonderful gizmo?" he asked doubtfully.

"Well . . ."

"Ah-ha! I rest my case." He sat back, a smug smile on his face.

Maggie leaned forward, peering at him across the table. "Wait a minute! Now I know why you look so familiar," she murmured, staring at his face. "I read this article in one of my old boss's trade magazines. . . ." Now what had that article said?

"You mean it wasn't my charisma and devastating good looks that captured your attention at the store?" he teased.

"Dream on," she replied. Although his assessment of her initial attraction to him was true, she didn't want him to know it. "I seem to remember something about you winning a court case, but I don't remember what it was about."

"Patents."

"Patents?" she asked, giving him a blank look.

"One of the gadgets I hold a patent on was being copied for production by another company," he explained.

"And they can't do that?" she asked, still unsure of what he meant.

"Not without my permission, for which they must pay me a princely sum," he explained with mock severity. "It's like owning a car: You can loan it to someone to use, or sell it to them, but if they just take it it's called stealing."

"Have you invented many things?" she asked, intrigued by what he did.

"Quite a few. Lately I've been working with face creams and hand lotions." Robert couldn't stop the smile that spread across his face as he noticed her obvious interest. He had her hooked. "But," he added, giving her a sly wink, "I'm not going to tell you anything else until our next date."

Maggie grinned back at him. She liked what she had seen of him so far, both his personality and his masculine attributes. He was interesting and she knew without a doubt that going out with him could be fun.

Why not? She needed some excitement in her life. "Okay, how about two weeks from this Friday?"

"Two weeks? You have a date every night for the next two weeks?" he asked incredulously.

She smiled at his expression, disbelieving and forlorn. "You don't think that's possible?"

"Very possible," he muttered, looking her over. "But when do you sleep and . . ." Robert's words trailed off uncomfortably, not liking where his thoughts were leading him. How could he feel so possessive about a woman he had just met? "Or do you sleep?" he asked her directly, not liking the knowing grin on her face either.

Maggie was tempted to let him stew for the next two weeks, but that wasn't her way. "Seriously, I'm working a lot of overtime this coming week. Then I'll go on the available list at the temporary service, and I like to stay close to the phone so I have first grab at the good assignments," she explained. "And," she added, picking up her purse, "I also have to be at work early tomorrow morning."

Robert paid the bill and followed her out of the restaurant. "Aren't you forgetting something?" he asked her expectantly when they arrived at her car.

"I don't kiss on the first date, Robert," she informed him in a wary tone.

"You wound me to the quick, Maggie," he said with a reproachful air. "You really do. I simply meant you forgot to give me your phone number." He smiled innocently as he held open her car door for her.

Maggie grinned up at him as she slipped behind the wheel. "You're inventive, Robert. I'm sure you can come up with it on your own." She started the engine, then rolled down the window a crack, unable to resist. "After all, how many Johnsons can there be in the phone book?"

He watched her leave, knowing he wasn't about to wait two weeks to see her again. His plan was already taking form. "You, Maggie Johnson," he said in a voice full of sensual promise, "are about to see just how inventive I really am."

CHAPTER TWO

Robert hesitated at the entrance to Alison Temporary, debating with himself for the third time that morning. Was this really such a good idea?

He did need help at the workshop. He was woefully behind in his entries to the daily logs he had to keep to authenticate his ownership of the various inventions he worked on. His files were a mess as well, and his commercial checking account was in a total state of chaos.

Then again, he had to be honest with himself. Maggie could almost certainly help him get organized—and he had to admit anything would be an improvement—but that wasn't the main reason he wanted to hire her. What he wanted was the opportunity to get to know her better. Hiring her would have them working closely together for some time to come, and he hoped that closeness could develop into a more personal relationship.

The trouble was, Maggie would most certainly insist on doing the job she was being hired for. Robert felt sure he could manage to mix business with pleasure, and was equally confident he could get her to do the same, but she seemed like the kind of person who would also take the business side of this blossoming relationship very seriously indeed. She would sort and file. She would organize his office. She would insist on efficiency.

And Robert simply wasn't sure he wanted his comfortably inefficient world tampered with, even by the lovely Maggie Johnson.

"Excuse me." The impatient feminine voice came from behind him, bringing him quickly back to reality.

"Oh, sorry." He opened the door to the temporary agency for the young woman and followed her in before he could change his mind.

"May I help you?" the receptionist asked.

"Well, um," he mumbled, glancing around nervously.

The room was small, tastefully decorated in muted pastels, the receptionist blending into the decor as if part of the planning. She looked quite efficient, her blond hair subdued, everything about her neat. Robert could envision Maggie taking on just such a professional air while on the job, and he again had doubts about his whole scheme. The trim blonde was looking at him expectantly.

"Are you looking for work?" she asked.

"Me? Um, no. I want to hire someone to work *for* me." There, the words were out. He sighed with relief when the receptionist nodded and smiled.

"Please have a seat," she said, all efficiency as she pulled out a printed sheet and looked at him. "In what capacity?" she inquired.

"I need someone to organize my office and books, catch my logs up, that sort of thing." He stifled a grin when he thought about some of the other duties he hoped to convince Maggie into taking on.

"Occupation?"

"I'm an inventor."

Though her perfectly outlined eyebrows arched slightly at that revelation, she continued to ask him the questions on her sheet, all the while dealing with ringing phones and directing people to various rooms. Robert continued to answer her, surprised by the thorough interrogation and relieved when it came to an end at last. He felt like he'd given his life history.

"Are all these questions necessary?" he asked.

"Yes." She stood up. "I'll be back in just a moment."

She disappeared into one of the offices, closing the door behind her. Robert shifted uncomfortably as he waited. How much more could they possibly need to know? All he wanted to do was hire one Maggie Johnson.

He decided it was just the nature of the business world to generate great piles of paperwork. That was part of the reason he was here in the first place. He hated the amount of work involved in trying to patent and keep his ideas safe, not to mention the tedious day-to-day tasks of simply running a business.

One of the office doors swung open and the receptionist emerged. "Ms. Clark will see you now," she informed him. "Her office is at the end of the hallway."

Robert got up and went in the direction she indicated, feeling somewhat trapped when she closed the door behind him as he made his way down the hall. Was it his imagination or did the passage seem to be getting narrower as he approached the last office? He knocked once on the door and went in, breathing a sigh of relief as he entered the spacious room.

"Mr. Langley, I'm Alison Clark," she said, reaching over her desk to shake his hand. "Please have a seat. Would you like something to drink?"

"No, thank you," Robert replied.

Alison Clark was an attractive woman in her mid-twenties, with shoulder-length black hair and a good figure. Robert was surprised she was so young. But she got right down to business.

"I see you've requested Maggie Johnson," she said, looking at him.

"Yes. She came highly recommended." He'd done his homework. After checking with all his business acquaintances, he'd found a friend who worked for a company where she'd been offered a permanent position, and he told Alison Clark his friend's name and company.

She nodded thoughtfully as she checked his explanation against the information sheet on her desk. "That company made her quite a lucrative offer to work there full-time. She turned them down."

"Do you know why?" Robert asked, trying to sound like a concerned prospective employer. It wasn't hard. He wanted to know as much about Maggie as he could.

Alison looked him over. The navy-blue chalk-stripe suit fitted him to perfection. He looked like he could have stepped out of a fashion magazine, not at all her idea of an inventor. "Evidently," she replied, "the position wasn't enough of a challenge for her."

"She won't have that problem with my office," Robert said, laughing openly. "It might even be too much for her."

"You don't know Maggie," she muttered to herself, then asked in a louder voice, "Do you have other employees?"

"No. I've had people working with me in the past, but not for the last few months." He looked at her intently. "Do you put every potential client through the same rigorous course, Ms. Clark?"

She cleared her throat. "To be honest, no. Most of the clients our agency deals with are corporations or small businesses." She crossed the room to pour herself a cup of coffee, offering him some by motion.

"Yes, please. Black." It looked like he might be here for a while longer than he'd intended. "So you're saying I'm some kind of a special case?" he inquired in an offended tone as she handed him his coffee.

"We can't be too careful these days, Mr. Langley," she said, slipping back behind her desk.

"Robert." He decided he'd better be nice to this lady. It occurred to him she could conceivably refuse to let him hire Maggie.

To his great relief she smiled, making her look even younger. "Alison," she returned.

"You own this agency?" he asked, trying not to sound too surprised so as not to offend her.

"My parents started it sometime ago and named it after me."

"Oh." Yes, he'd better be *very* nice to her.

"You see, Robert, you don't have any other employees, your business is in a remote warehouse location, you've requested one of my best temps, who also happens to be one of the most attractive women we have working for us, and—"

He held up his hands to cut her off. "Okay, I surrender," he announced, laughing contritely. "Shall I dump coffee in my own lap for being such a pain, or would you like to do the honors?"

Alison laughed, too, amused by the unusual man before her. He was holding his coffee cup over his head, ready to pour it on himself. "I don't think that's necessary, Robert."

"I'm so relieved. My housekeeper already thinks I'm a total mess. I'm not sure she'd believe my explanations this time."

"This time?" she asked, her curiosity aroused.

"Occasionally some of my experiments have a tendency to, um, explode." He saw her eyebrows arch in alarm and realized he'd made a big mistake.

"Explode?"

"Erupt would be a better word," Robert added hastily. "Not at all dangerous, I assure you. Just messy."

She continued to look at him with a great deal of skepticism, obviously unsure whether to believe him or not. "Does this happen very often?"

"No, not in the last few weeks anyway," he murmured. "But I want to assure you that Maggie —Ms. Johnson won't be in any danger. My workshop is located away from the office area. She—"

"Robert," Alison interrupted, "the decision to work for you is up to Ms. Johnson. She has the right to refuse any job, and if she starts one and doesn't want to continue with it, she doesn't have to."

"That makes sense." He liked that kind of freedom himself. It did, however, present a problem in this case. He would have to win Maggie's trust, convince her he was serious about employing her before moving to more personal ground. Still . . .

"She'll be finished with the job she's on this Friday," Alison informed him. "I don't know yet whether Ms. Johnson intends to take on another job right away or take some time off." She slipped some papers into a file. "When do you need her to start?"

"As soon as possible," he answered, breathing a silent sigh of relief. He'd thought he'd really blown it, mentioning the experiments.

"I'll let you know her decision."

"Thank you, Alison." He stood up and shook her hand. "I appreciate your thoroughness."

And with that he took his leave before he put his foot in his mouth again. He also couldn't wait to get out of his suit. His housekeeper, Inez, must be mad at him again; his shirt was starched stiff as a board.

But he'd done it. With any luck at all, on Monday next Maggie would be working for him. Of course, he would have to move slowly, gradually involve her in his business affairs before letting her know he was interested in a different kind of affair.

Patience. He would have to exercise patience. It wouldn't be easy. He called to mind Maggie's soft voice, gorgeous hazel eyes, and delicious figure. No, it wouldn't be easy, but he had the feeling she would be well worth the effort.

"Nancy, would you please call Maggie Johnson and tell her to meet me for lunch? She'll know where."

Alison's gut instinct was to trust Robert Langley, but something wasn't right here. Maggie wasn't just her best temp, she was a friend. And though it wasn't unusual for a client to request a particular worker, this Langley character seemed a bit too anxious. It was probably all quite innocent, but there was no harm in double-checking everything just in case there was more to this job than met the eye.

In the cozy little restaurant that was a common meeting place for Alison Temporary workers, Maggie watched her friend push salad around her plate without eating so much as a bite.

"Okay, Ali," Maggie said when she could stand it no longer. "Fess up. What's wrong?"

The young woman chuckled. "You know me too well."

"Is something wrong at the agency?"

"Oh, no, everything's great. Mom and Dad are due back in two weeks, though, and I can't wait." She finally took a bite of her salad and chewed slowly. "I really miss going out on different assignments. Running the agency is hard work and they can keep it." She grimaced at her friend. "I haven't been out on a date in over a month!"

Maggie smiled, waiting for her to get to the real reason behind this luncheon date. Alison was the one who had first encouraged Maggie to quit her old job and begin working for her parents' temporary services agency. It hadn't taken all that much prompting, really. She had hated her boss, had been dissatisfied with her job at Chapman Corporation for some time, and had just been biding her time and trying to decide what to move on to.

The temporary assignments were perfect for her.

35

Her life had fallen into such a dull routine. Now, she didn't know what each week would bring and was enjoying herself immensely. Still, she harbored a desire to find something she could really sink her teeth into somewhere along the way. A challenge, that's what she needed.

"Speaking of dates, how's *your* social life, Maggie?" Alison asked, trying to appear casual. "Met any new, exciting men lately?"

"Honestly, Ali, you're worse than both our mothers!" Maggie exclaimed, shaking her head.

Her friend leaned across the table and shook her fork at her. "I won't be put off. Give!"

"Well, I did meet someone at that department store job Sunday evening," Maggie admitted hesitantly. "He's, um, interesting. We're going out in two weeks."

"Two weeks? Why so long?" Ali demanded. This sounded too much like her own lackluster social life.

She smiled knowingly at her. "You know how many hours I've put in lately. I don't have time to date right now." The excuse sounded lame even to her, so she abruptly changed the subject. "What happened to Tom?" she asked, referring to the last person she could remember Ali dating.

"He's been out of town, but things were cooling off before he left." Alison sighed forlornly. "This is too depressing. Let's move on to something really interesting." Rubbing her hands together, she announced, "Dessert time!"

They talked about people they both knew and Maggie's present job while consuming rich chocolate mousse. Finally, though, Alison got down to discussing her unusual visitor that morning.

"I have another job for you," she said abruptly.

"Already?"

"As always, you don't have to take it if you don't want to, but he, um . . ." Alison cleared her throat and looked slyly at Maggie. "He requested you personally."

Maggie arched her eyebrows in surprise. "Who?"

"An inventor. It sounds like a real challenge too." She grinned, looking mischievous. "He's easy on the eyes."

Her mouth dropping open, Maggie stared at her friend incredulously, too surprised to speak.

"Seems like a nice guy too," Alison continued. "His name is—"

"Robert Langley," Maggie completed.

"I knew it!" her friend cried in triumph. "I knew there was more to this request than he let on. Come on, tell me all the juicy details."

Fighting a very unaccustomed blush, Maggie tried to regain her composure. "There's nothing to tell. Absolutely nothing. He's the one I met at the store."

"The plot thickens!"

"Stop that! We had coffee, talked a bit. Like you said, he seems pretty nice and—" Why on earth would he want her to work for him? "What exactly did he say?"

"Just that he needed you to help him organize his office, file work and such," Alison replied with a shrug. The gleam remained in her eyes. "How does it feel to be needed by a man like him?"

"Why me?" Maggie asked, ignoring her not-so-subtle innuendo.

Alison shrugged again. "Maybe he decided you were the only woman for the job, Maggie dear," she replied in a teasing tone.

Maggie shook a warning finger at her. "Ali . . ."

"Really, he does have an unusual occupation. I suppose he just felt comfortable with you and decided you could do the job without interrupting his creative processes or whatever," she went on reasonably. "I mean, you must have hit it off, right?"

"I suppose." Maggie wasn't so sure. "It just seems a bit odd, that's all." She remembered the mutual attraction they felt for one another.

"Like I said, you don't have to take it. Although," Ali added in a conspiratorial tone, "I think you'd be a fool to turn it down."

"Why?"

"Aren't you the one looking for something different? A challenge? A job you can really sink your teeth into?" she asked. "What could be more different than working for an inventor?"

"Yes, but—"

Alison patted her hand and winked at her. "If it

38

turns out to be more than you can handle, you could always recommend me for the position."

"Some friend you are," Maggie returned dryly. "You're ready to take him away from me before I even start."

"Him? I thought we were talking about a job."

Maggie looked heavenward, cursing her inadvertent slip of the tongue. "We are," she said, trying to convince herself as well as Alison. "Just a job."

"You don't fool me for a minute, Maggie Johnson," she declared, watching her friend carefully.

"And you know my feelings about romance in the work place," Maggie said.

"Maybe you just haven't found the right office yet. Or," she added with a smile, "the right guy."

"Ali!"

Alison's expression suddenly turned from teasing to businesslike. "Are you going to take the job or not?"

"I suppose," Maggie replied nonchalantly, trying not to examine her motives for taking the job too closely. "I do need another assignment come Monday, and this might be an interesting change of pace." She picked up her purse, put her half of the lunch tab and tip on the table, then stood to leave. "Even if you don't have to be back," she teased, "this working girl does."

"But—"

"Sorry, Ali, I'm going to be late if I don't leave

right now. You can inform Robert Langley that he's just hired himself a temporary worker."

And that was all he'd hired, Maggie thought as she walked quickly back to work. Robert was in for a surprise if his request for her organizational skills was nothing more than a smoke screen to cover up a planned seduction. She was quite serious about her work. If he didn't really need her help she'd be out the door in a flash.

On the other hand, if he did need her help and was serious about their working relationship, this assignment could turn out to be just what she was looking for. Ali was right. What could be more different than working for an inventor? Especially a handsome, successful, very masculine inventor like Robert Langley.

Who was she trying to fool? Robert hadn't requested her by accident. Maybe he did honestly feel she was the right woman for the job, but he had ulterior motives as well and she knew it. She also knew how much she was attracted to him. No doubt about it, sparks were going to fly. What worried her the most was how much she was looking forward to the fireworks.

CHAPTER THREE

On the information sheet from Alison Temporary, Robert had called his place of business a workshop. What it turned out to be was a warehouse, set off by itself on the southwest side of town. It was a nice-looking building, fairly new, with a surprising number of windows. A decent attempt had been made to landscape the grounds around it and to conceal its prefabricated concrete construction.

But a warehouse was a warehouse in Maggie's opinion. She'd seen enough of the tiny, so-called offices people usually partitioned off inside them to be wary of what Robert's working environment would be like. The remote location didn't exactly tickle her either.

If she screamed for help, nobody would hear her.

"Now you're being silly," she chided herself as she pulled into the parking lot beside the building. She took a deep breath, blew it out in a here-goes-nothing sigh, and got out of her car.

Inside, Robert breathed a sigh, too; his, however, was one of sheer relief. He had been pacing around his cluttered office, occasionally kicking something out of his way in frustration, nearly convinced Maggie wasn't going to show up. Now that she had, he was suddenly panic-stricken that she would take one look at this mess and leave.

Crossing anxiously to the window, he looked out and watched as Maggie locked her car. Should he go out to meet her or wait for her to come in? He'd best not appear too eager, he decided. He settled for hitting a button by his desk, automatically opening the sliding glass doors downstairs.

Maggie halted in her tracks when the doors leading into the warehouse opened of their own accord, remembering a bit of a nursery rhyme. " 'Come into my parlor, said the spider to the fly,' " she muttered under her breath.

After her initial doubt had subsided, she hadn't had a second thought about accepting this assignment—until now, at least. But she summoned her courage and stepped through the doors. After all, Robert was an inventor, probably loved gadgets, and that was all there was to this unusual greeting. He had her intrigued and she intended to satisfy her curiosity one way or the other.

A sign in front of her read OFFICE in big red letters, with an arrow indicating a flight of stairs to one side. She climbed them, her footsteps echoing off the walls of the cavernous building, wondering why Robert hadn't met her. Was this a ruse, a way of showing her right off the bat that he was the boss?

At the top of the stairs another sign directed her to the left so she walked that way, her pace slowing when she saw an open door up ahead. She peeked inside. Her eyes widened. It was all she could do to prevent herself from turning and taking off at a dead run.

Maggie couldn't believe what she saw. If she wanted a challenge, she certainly had one. Papers stacked upon papers covered every surface—and there were plenty of surfaces. Tables, desks, most of the chairs—in some spots she couldn't even see the floor. Lord, what had she gotten herself into? Before, she had worried about being cooped up in some tiny cubicle; now, she'd give anything for that to be true. The room was huge.

"Hello, Maggie."

Robert smiled at the expression on her face, knowing the office came as a shock. That's why he had decided to meet her here instead of at the front door. This way she would have something to concentrate on other than him and the way he had gone about employing her. It seemed to be working.

She turned in the direction of his voice and saw him standing beside a row of filing cabinets. She wondered if they had anything in them.

"Hello, Robert," she said.

It was a good thing she was numb from the enormity of the task before her, because she hadn't

43

anticipated the way she'd feel when she saw him again. He looked as good as she remembered. Jeans hugged his strong thighs and a fawn chamois shirt covered his broad chest. And then there were his gray eyes, looking at her with frank masculine appraisal.

"Ready to start work?"

"That depends." Maggie looked pointedly around the room, managing to salvage her composure and trying desperately to do the same with her sense of humor. "When does the bulldozer arrive?"

He grinned sheepishly. "It is a little messy."

"That's like saying the garbage dump is a little dirty!" she cried in disbelief. "When was the last time someone actually did any filing around here?"

"Well . . ."

"Perhaps I should explain. By filing I mean putting papers in a folder and then into an alphabetically arranged cabinet."

Robert bristled at her patronizing tone. "I know what it means." The trouble was, he honestly couldn't remember the last time he'd done any.

"If you have to think about it, it's too long." She looked down at her border print skirt, black pumps, and new taupe blouse, then looked at him and shook her head. "I have to go home."

"Wait! I thought you wanted a challenge."

"I do." He needed her help all right, but she decided to let him stew a little. "This, however, goes way beyond a challenge! It—it—"

44

"Leaves you speechless?"

Maggie nodded. "How do you find anything in here?"

"I have a system," he replied defensively.

"When did looking for a needle in a haystack become a system?" she asked.

"It's not that bad."

"It's worse." She looked around again, trying to get used to the disorder. "Forget filing for a moment. When was the last time someone worked in here at all?"

"Hmm. I had an assistant a while back. Craig Smith. I wouldn't call what he did work, though." Should he lie or give it to her straight? "A while."

"Could you be a little more specific?"

"Why?"

"If," she said, looking at him pointedly, "I repeat, *if* I take this job on I'd like to know what I'm getting myself into."

There was no use beating around the bush. She would find out anyway—if she stayed. "Three weeks, I believe."

"You managed to make this mess in just three weeks?" she asked incredulously.

"I know where everything is," he informed her haughtily.

She'd heard that one before. "Is that so? In that case, name a file."

"Excuse me?"

"Give me the name of a file you're working with."

Robert cleared his throat uncertainly. "Dandy." At least he thought he knew where that one was.

"That's the name of a file?" she asked, rolling her eyes.

"So sue me," he returned with a shrug. "I didn't name the company. I'm just working on something for them."

"Find it for me," she requested, then added, "please?" After all, he was supposed to be the boss.

Robert walked confidently over to the table nearest the coffee machine and looked down, trying to hide his consternation as he sifted through the piles of papers. The file wasn't there, and for the life of him he couldn't remember having moved it. Then he heard Maggie chuckle.

He turned around slowly, seeing her leaning against the filing cabinets holding a bunch of papers in her hand. His healthy complexion darkened slightly.

"Dandy, right?" she asked smugly, waving the papers at him.

Robert sighed in exasperation. "Now I remember. I left them there last night so I could find them easily in the morning." He lifted his chin defiantly. "I told you I knew where everything was."

Maggie grinned. She would have laughed, but decided changing the subject would be a wiser course of action. He didn't look one bit amused. "Why did the last person quit?"

"Just a minute," Robert shot back. "I'm supposed to be interviewing you for this job, remember?"

"Answer the question."

If he answered it truthfully, she might very well turn and walk out. That would mean he'd have to return to the normal route with her, ask her out for a date and go from there. He didn't have the time or patience for that kind of lengthy courtship. Not only that, he knew he needed help around here and needed it soon.

"She didn't like all the work."

Maggie shook her head. "You pay too well. There has to be something else." She gazed at him suspiciously.

"She didn't like the job."

"Robert," Maggie said ominously, "I am flattered you requested me personally, and although I have my doubts about working with a man who could have created this—this secretary's nightmare," she added, waving at the mess, "I think I can help you. But I will not take the job until you tell me why your former helper left."

"Oh, all right." He'd hoped to get around this. "There was a minor explosion."

"An explosion!" Maggie gasped.

"Just a tiny one. Rattled the windows, maybe shook her around a little bit," he said hastily. By the look of disbelief on Maggie's face he could tell she wasn't reassured. "But I've given up on that project." He gave her a winning smile. "I'm working on something else now."

"Does it explode?"

"It hasn't yet," he replied cheerfully.

Maggie gave him an assessing look, picked up her purse, and turned toward the door. She could practically feel his desperation, could definitely hear it in his voice.

"Where are you going?"

"Home."

"But—"

"To change my clothes," she continued, grinning at his crestfallen expression. "Don't worry. This looks like too much of a challenge for me to pass up. Besides, maybe I can get Alison to squeeze hazardous duty pay out of you."

Robert sighed in relief, then looked her over with a roguish smile. "I like what you have on."

"Robert Langley, I'm not about to work in this mess wearing anything nicer than my grubbiest jeans." In view of his revelation about explosions, perhaps she'd buy a hard hat as well.

"Oh." The thought of seeing her in a pair of tight jeans quickened his pulse. He smiled. "Maggie?"

"Yes?" She turned around to look at him.

"Could you please buy some coffee while you're out?"

She looked at the empty pot and back to him, shaking her head. "I don't know about this, Robert. We'll give it a day or two and see what happens."

"That's all I'm asking, Maggie," he replied innocently. He watched the delicious swing of her hips as she left the office. "For now."

When Maggie returned, Robert wasn't in the office. But she could hear strange noises coming from somewhere in the building and decided he was off doing whatever it was he did. Though curious, the thought of walking into the middle of an explosion didn't thrill her, so she stayed where she was.

"Maybe the smell of fresh coffee will bring him running," she mumbled. Looking at the mess again, she knew she needed it. Lots of it.

First she had to clean the pot, and found that to do so required clearing the bathroom sink of empty coffee cups, making her feel more like a janitor at the moment than the efficient secretary she was. At last she had coffee brewing and the aroma did indeed bring Robert up from his work, whereupon Maggie promptly confronted him.

"We're going to have to have a little talk about the division of labor around here," she told him curtly. "I'm a secretary, not a scullery maid. I don't mind making the coffee because I drink it, too, but *you* are hereby appointed chief dishwasher."

"Now just a minute," Robert said, taken aback by her sudden ferocity. All he'd wanted was a cup of coffee. "I—"

"And while we're on the subject," Maggie interrupted, "I don't do windows, mop floors, dust, or

take out the garbage. I know a very good maintenance firm I can call if you wish."

"For your information I already have one," he
replied briskly. "It's just that I have them on a per
call basis because I don't like them messing around
here when I'm in the middle of a project."

"Oh." Maggie took one look at the anger in his
eyes and realized she had overstepped her bounds.
"All right. I was simply setting the ground rules. I
guess I got carried away."

Robert went to the coffeepot and poured himself
a cup. It tasted marvelous, but in his present mood
he refused to compliment her. Maybe this working
together wasn't such a good idea after all. "Is there
anything else that doesn't fall under your job description?" he asked warily.

"That's about it," she replied. She sighed and
took a sip of her own coffee, wondering why she'd
jumped all over him. Maybe it was the fact that
just being near him had her nerve endings tingling.
"I'm sorry, Robert. It's just that I never know
what to expect when I start a new job. Would you
believe one of my old bosses actually wanted me to
pick up his dry cleaning for him?"

"Really?" Robert cleared his throat, making a
mental note that he'd have to pick up his shirts
tonight himself. His housekeeper couldn't come
back from vacation soon enough for him.

"Really. One guy even wanted me to do his grocery shopping for him. As long as I was going to
the store anyway, he said. Can you imagine?"

Robert laughed, suddenly feeling superior. At least he hadn't even considered that. Then his smile disappeared. "Um, what do I owe you for the coffee?" he asked contritely.

"Oh, Robert. I didn't mind that," Maggie assured him when she saw the stricken look on his face. "That falls under the heading of office supplies as far as I'm concerned." Laughing, she crossed the room and handed him a receipt. "Here. I bought some file folders and labels too."

"Thanks. If it counts for anything, Maggie, I'd never ask you to clean up around here. Once you restore some semblance of order so they won't throw anything important away, I'll call the maintenance crew. Okay?"

"Okay," she replied, returning his warm smile. "And it counts, Robert. Thanks."

"So. Where do you plan to start?"

She joined him in surveying the clutter. "How about a nice bonfire?"

"Hey!"

"Just kidding. I'm going to try to sort the big piles into smaller piles and then set up a filing system," she explained. "Any particular method you'd like?"

"What's wrong with the one I've been using?"

"Toss and pray?"

He did his best to ignore the sarcasm in her tone. "I meant alphabetical."

"Well, of course." Maggie did her best not to laugh out loud. "But from there one usually sets up subheadings. File name, company name, date of project beginning or completion—something like that."

Robert looked at her, enjoying the sparkling light of intelligence in her warm hazel eyes. "I know when I'm out of my depth. You do what you think best as long as I can find things when I need them—or, rather, so *you* can find them when I need them."

"Careful," she warned him with a mischievous grin. "It has been known for a secretary to set up a filing system in such a way as to ensure job security."

"You mean so that nobody can find a thing without her?"

"Exactly."

He gazed at her speculatively. "I'll take my chances."

"You've been warned."

She winked at him, poured herself another cup of coffee, then went to the desk to attack the task at hand. Robert got some more coffee, too, then stood watching her for a moment, enjoying the way she moved, the way her hair swirled around her face when she bent over to look at something.

His observation finally made Maggie self-conscious and she looked up from her sorting, tucking her hair behind one ear and fixing him with a questioning gaze.

"Well?" she asked impatiently.

"Excuse me?"

"I have work to do, and I assume you have some as well or you'd never be able to afford my fee."

Robert chuckled. "I do. I was just watching the beauty of efficiency." His eyes dipped to her thighs, tightly encased in faded blue jeans. "Or is that the efficiency of beauty?" he added slyly.

"Shoo!" Maggie exclaimed, waving him out of the room before his perusal of her feminine attributes could make her blush. "Go invent something!"

"Good idea."

His laughter faded as he strolled down the hall. To Maggie his laugh sounded just a little bit evil, but she was soon too immersed in her work to worry.

Though relieved to find that Robert took his work very seriously indeed, Maggie still chided him—from a safe distance, of course—for not breaking for lunch. She left the chicken salad sandwich he ordered in a bag at the foot of the stairs for him and went back to work, feeling as if she'd done her duty. The bag was gone the next time she looked.

Now she was crawling around on the floor, sorting papers, trying to give some order to what she had come to refer to as the Langley Landslide. She sat back on her heels and took stock of the situation.

"Well, now. Twenty-six piles. That's a start."

She frowned, realizing she was talking out loud again. "Bad sign, Maggie. Get a grip on yourself."

Stepping out of the circle, she gathered up another pile of papers and overstuffed file folders, then sank to her knees to begin the process again. *"A, B, C.* I really should have brought some knee pads with me." The floor was carpeted, but crawling around the circle distributing material to the appropriate piles was taking its toll.

She was so absorbed she didn't see Robert leaning against the doorjamb, thoroughly enjoying the view before him. Maggie had her derriere in the air as she hunched over a pile of papers. Every now and then her shapely rear end would wiggle invitingly.

He hadn't been wrong about her body; from this angle she looked great. Better than great. The sudden masculine stirrings within him testified to his desire, and the fact he was able to stand here without pouncing on her spoke well of his willpower. For the moment at least he would be able to live up to his vow of earning her trust before pressing on to a more intimate acquaintance.

"Blast it!"

Robert sighed. He was enjoying the show, but decided it was time to make his presence known. "Is something wrong?"

Maggie sat back on her heels and glared at him over her shoulder. "Something? Try everything."

"Can I help?" he asked, walking up to the edge of her self-imposed paper prison.

"Don't step on anything!" she warned, then held out a sheet of paper to him. "What's this?"

Stepping carefully into her circle, he glanced at the paper in her hand. "I'm not sure."

"Great. If you don't know, who does?"

"Just give me a minute to remember." He sat down beside her, frowning as he read the document. "It must be part of the Slippery project." He leaned closer to her, his thigh pressing against hers as he returned the sheet.

"The Slippery project?" Maggie muttered. "That's an appropriate name. This whole mess is a slippery project." She continued to utter exasperated epithets under her breath as she put the paper in question into the correctly labeled folder. "And how about this one?" she asked, holding up another suspect document.

He leaned still closer. She appreciated his help—in fact needed it desperately at this point—but did he have to sit so close? She could feel the heat of his body next to hers, tempting her, making her very much aware of her attraction to him.

Robert looked at the paper he held in his hand, trying to concentrate on the printed page. The scent she wore was both sensuous and intoxicating. He'd love to nuzzle her neck, nibble on the delicate skin exposed above her plaid shirt. He looked up at her eyes and found her gazing at him expectantly.

"Well?"

"Oh." He cleared his throat, noticing his voice was getting a bit hoarse. "Yes, that goes over here,

I believe." He leaned across her, inadvertently brushing her breasts with his arm. They were so soft and full he couldn't stop himself from brushing them again on his way back.

A soft gasp escaped her before she could prevent the telltale sound. She didn't think he'd done it on purpose, but his simple touch had sent liquid heat running through her traitorous body.

"And this one?" she asked, not daring to look into his startling gray eyes as she handed the paper to him.

"Hmm." He ignored the file she was holding out to him. The graceful line of her neck was exposed as she added something to another pile. He couldn't resist; her silky skin was calling out to him. Did she feel as smooth as she looked? One little touch wouldn't scare her off. . . .

"Robert!" she exclaimed, jerking away from him and dropping the file in his lap.

Trailing one finger along her jawline and down her throat, he watched as a delicate pink color washed over her face. "Yes, Maggie?" he murmured.

"This is a business," she said in a scolding tone, trying to move away from him, "not a singles' bar."

His wandering finger paused at the opening of her shirt. She felt frozen in time. Her body wanted him to continue and it was overruling her mind, her nipples taut and straining for attention. Just a slight movement and he would be touching her breasts. Was it her imagination or did she already feel the intimate caress?

"Robert . . ."

"Hmm?" Sliding his hand around her neck, he pulled her closer to him. His lips were almost touching hers, and yet something held him back.

She could feel his warm breath on her cheek and knew she wanted him to kiss her. In an unconscious action she leaned closer to him and their lips met, her mind whirling with surprise to find his not hard and hungry but soft and yielding. When she started swaying slightly against him, Robert caught her and pulled her close.

He tasted her as if she was a fine wine, delicately sipping at the treasure before him. Her lips opened to his insistent probing, and she reveled in the silky texture of his tongue as it tangled with hers. Pleasure and desire surged through her body, threatening to overwhelm her.

Maggie knew she should stop this. It was insane and so out of character for her. He was her boss and she his employee. Yet it had happened and she was glad, loved the feel of his hard chest pressing against her breasts.

Her boss! She pushed away from him at the thought. Breathing deeply, she tried to pull herself together, not daring to look at him. How could she have let this happen? She had warned herself when she took this job that she was too susceptible to his touch.

"Maggie," he said softly, "look at me."

She wasn't about to face him until she had complete control of her emotions. Breathing deeply, she was at last able to ask him, "Is this how you treat all your employees?"

"Hardly. And you know it." He lifted her hair and slipped it behind her shell-like ear. "But there's something special between us, Maggie. Don't try to deny that you feel it too."

"I'm being paid to do a secretarial job here," she said, brushing off his touch. "Nothing else."

"I didn't force you. I distinctly remember giving you time to change your mind." He looked at her, caressing her cheek as he turned her face to his. "And you were the one who gave in first, not me."

"It won't happen again," she informed him, moving away from his tempting grasp.

"No, not like this."

Next time he fully intended to go a lot farther than a simple kiss. For now, though, he realized he had to return to being patient, even though this glimpse of her passionate nature would make biding his time harder than ever. But he could do it, just as he had been able to stay clear of her all day. Slow and easy, he thought, one step at a time until she went willingly into his arms.

"Do you have an iron, Maggie?" he asked in a conversational tone. The first thing he had to do was put her at ease.

"What?" She looked at him, puzzled, trying to figure out what he was up to now.

"Along with our slip in professional etiquette,

there appears to be another casualty here," he replied, holding out the file she had dropped into his lap earlier.

Their slip? Was he trying to say he had simply gotten carried away, just as she had? He seemed almost as anxious as she to forget what had just happened and get back to work. Whatever his motive, it was a way out, and she took it.

She examined the somewhat crumpled file he held out to her. "It doesn't look any worse than some of the others I've found today."

"Maggie, you wound me," he said, smiling at her. "But I suppose you're right. Neither my files nor my willpower are starched to perfection."

"I guess you're not alone in the wilted willpower department," she admitted. There was no use denying they were attracted to one another. But it appeared Robert shared her concern over romance in the office. "As to your files," she added dryly, glad things were returning to normal, "I'm afraid even starch and ironing aren't enough to straighten those out."

There. Her tension was disappearing. He returned her friendly, teasing smile. "I beg your pardon!"

"Don't give me that 'who me?' look," Maggie returned, standing up and slipping to safety behind a desk. She still didn't trust him, and she knew better now than to trust herself. She sat down well out of his reach. "I have a few more unidentified objects here," she informed him.

Robert shrugged and got to his feet, careful not to approach her. "Then let's identify them."

"Here." She pushed a sheaf of papers across the desk. "What, pray tell, are these?"

"More of the aptly named Slippery file." He added it to the folder. "By the way, did I mention my checking account?"

"No, you didn't." She looked at him warily. "Why?"

"I keep getting these letters from the bank," he replied, looking on top of another desk. "They're around here somewhere. . . ."

"When was the last time you balanced your account?"

"Never," he mumbled. "I found them!" he exclaimed, holding the bank envelopes up triumphantly.

"Never?" She looked at the pile he placed on her desk, then up at him in amazement. "You haven't even opened these."

"I figured if it was really important they'd call me," he explained honestly.

Maggie looked heavenward, wondering where he possibly could have come from. A pumpkin patch perhaps, or maybe a home for the hopelessly unorganized? "You've really never balanced your checking account?"

"I refuse to answer that on the grounds it might tend to embarrass me," he replied amiably, turning to search still another pile. "You have to understand that up until a year ago my sister worked for

60

me. She took care of all this." He came back with some more envelopes. "Her husband was transferred to Europe and she couldn't wait to leave me."

"I can't imagine why," Maggie observed dryly. "Did you renew this CD?" she asked after opening the first envelope.

"I don't know."

She sighed. "Who would know?"

"Maybe my accountant." He looked at her quizzically, then smiled. "If not, I'm sure the bank—"

"Never mind." Maggie shook her head in disbelief. She bent down and picked up a large, oversized leather-bound book from a stack of similar volumes on the floor. "While I have you here, what are these?"

"My daily logs."

"Daily?"

"They're to be kept up daily, to support my documentation on patents I apply for."

"In that case, we've got a problem with them," she said, glancing at the last reference. It had been made more than three weeks ago.

Robert liked the way she put that. His problems were becoming her problems too. "I know. We'll get them all caught up soon," he said confidently.

"One last question before I call it a day."

"Shoot."

"Have those filing cabinets ever been used?"

"Off and on." He sighed dramatically. "You

61

know how it is, Maggie. It's so hard to get good help these days."

She fixed him with a murderous gaze. "Isn't it though?"

He smiled at her, not the least bit bothered by her sarcasm. "I want to show you how the door works before you leave tonight. I'm not always here in the morning."

He showed her the button that opened the heavy sliding glass doors on the first floor, then gave her something that looked like a credit card and took her downstairs to show her how to use it.

"Magnetically coded," he informed her.

"What happens when you have unexpected visitors?"

"I don't have unexpected visitors. I'm an inventor, remember?" He looked around the deserted parking lot and added in a whisper, "We wouldn't want anybody stealing our secrets, now would we?"

"I don't know what you're worried about," Maggie returned. "Even if they got in I don't see how they'd find any secrets to steal. As a matter of fact, they'd probably get buried under the rubble and never be heard from again."

Robert laughed merrily as he escorted her out to her car. "Come on, Maggie, admit it. You like working here. It's a challenge, right?"

"Hmm," she replied doubtfully, but she was smiling.

She did like working for him. It was certainly a

challenge, one she wouldn't feel right about walking away from. Nor could she walk away from a man who needed her help so desperately. In spite of the momentary slip in professional etiquette, as Robert had described their kiss earlier, Maggie also felt she could handle the growing attraction she felt for him. That, too, was a challenge she couldn't turn down.

He opened the car door for her. "By the way, where would you like to go on our date this Friday?" he inquired casually.

"Our what?" She turned to face him, her smile gone.

"Our date. I'll pick you up at seven."

"Oh, no, you won't. I have a very strict policy against dating bosses and fellow employees." She wasn't about to go out with him. After what happened earlier she could just imagine what the consequences would be if they were alone in a more romantic setting.

"I've already waited one whole week for you," he said, ignoring her objections. "I'm really looking forward to this weekend."

She didn't like the way he said that. "No."

"Maggie—"

"No. That's *n-o,*" she enunciated carefully. "Read my lips."

Robert decided he'd rather kiss them than read them, but he asked, "Why not?"

"You already know my reasons."

"Don't be silly," he chided softly. "Just because

you work for me doesn't mean we can't be friends." He wanted much more than that, but friendship would do for a start.

"You know as well as I do that—"

"That we can't keep our hands off each other?" Robert completed.

"That's not so!" she objected vehemently. The trouble was, that was exactly what she was worried about. Obviously, Robert was well aware of her doubts.

"Afraid, Maggie?"

"No."

"Then go out with me."

"I can't, it's—"

"I won't hurt you, Maggie," he said, reaching out to cup her face in his hand, "ever."

His gentle touch was sending tingling sensations coursing through her body. She wanted to go out with him, get to know him better. But he was her boss and she was enjoying her work. Where would all this lead?

"You promised," he reminded her, stroking her cheek with his thumb. "Do you always break your promises?"

"No, I don't." Continuing to fight would only make him grow more insistent. And she had promised. Looking up at him, she knew she was about to give in. "One date."

"To begin with," he said, releasing her so she could get into her car. By the time she rolled down her window he was already walking away.

"Only one, Robert Langley," she yelled to his retreating back. His only answer before disappearing into the warehouse was a hearty masculine laugh.

CHAPTER FOUR

It was a lovely morning. The sun shining in a cloudless sky was warm upon Maggie's skin as she crossed the parking lot to the warehouse. A light breeze was blowing from the south, carrying with it the delicious smell of earth and green, growing plants still moist with dew.

She felt good, optimistic, filled with a sense of purpose and direction she hadn't really had in quite some time. Organizing the Langley Landslide into an efficient, smooth-running system was more than just a challenge to her; it was her opportunity to virtually create her own working environment, implement her own ideas on how an office should be run instead of being forced to work within someone else's plan. Maggie knew the task would be a test of her abilities, and she welcomed it with open arms.

There were problems, of course, like the insane attraction she had for her boss and the equally insane date she had agreed to yesterday. But Maggie felt confident she could contain her attraction for

Robert and keep their upcoming date within the bounds of a friendly working relationship.

She wasn't fooling herself, however. Despite his assurances, she knew Robert had more on his mind than friendship. And to be honest, when he was near her, Maggie had some pretty alarming desires herself. The path before her seemed clear: Just as she would have to convince him her way of organization was the best way, she would also have to convince him there was only one way for a boss and employee to behave.

"The three *P*'s," she said to herself, smiling as she inserted her magnetic card into the door lock. "Polite, professional, and platonic."

As if to mock her thoughts, Maggie was greeted by Robert's raucous laughter as soon as she entered the building. Curious, she threw caution to the wind and followed the sound of his chuckling.

The first floor of the warehouse had been partitioned into what appeared to Maggie to be a higgledy-piggledy system of workshops, with walls and interconnecting doors but no ceilings. Each massive space seemed to have a specific function, such as the metal and woodworking shops she passed through as she searched for Robert. The one she found him in looked something like a chemist's laboratory, with gas burners, test tubes, and cabinets filled with odd-looking compounds in flasks.

"You'll have to work on that laugh," she told

him, still unable to see what had him so amused. "A mad scientist should cackle, not chuckle."

Standing at a waist-high table, a white lab coat covering his street clothes, Robert turned his head and looked at her over his shoulder. His expression was a mixture of consternation and relief.

"Maggie! Thank heavens you're here." He turned his head back around, looking at the table in front of him. "At least I think I'm glad you're here."

"What's wrong?" she asked, wondering why he was standing in such an odd position. His hips were pressed up against the worktable, and when he looked at her again he still didn't turn to face her.

"Um, I seem to have glued myself to this worktable," he muttered, his complexion a bit redder than usual.

"You're kidding!" Maggie moved closer, looking at the point where his clothing touched the table. He did indeed appear to be stuck fast to the metal surface. She started laughing. "W-what have you invented?" she sputtered. "The magnetic, um, personality?"

"Very funny," Robert grumbled, but he managed a wry grin and shrugged his shoulders. "Actually, I was just using some special glue to mount a test tube into this apparatus," he explained, indicating a bizarre-looking tangle of glass tubes, vials, and steel clamps. "The glue applicator got away from me and . . . well, I guess you can see for yourself what happened."

Maggie tried to look sympathetic, but she kept chuckling in spite of herself as he wriggled like an insect stuck to flypaper. "I guess it's a good thing I didn't decide this job was too much for me and quit, isn't it? I mean, what would you have done if I hadn't shown up?"

"The stuff doesn't work too well at bonding a porous material like cloth to metal," he said, ignoring her astute assessment of his predicament, "and I managed to pull my lab coat and pants free, but . . ."

She peered at the area in question and started laughing anew. "You're stuck by your zipper!"

"There's still some glue left," Robert warned her in a vindictive tone. "I could always glue your lips together."

"You're hardly in a position to make threats, Robert," she reminded him. She smiled sweetly and glanced at her watch. "I think I'll take my coffee break now."

His eyes widened when she turned to leave. "Maggie!"

"Yes, sir?" she said in her best secretarial voice.

"If I'm stuck here I can't sign your pay voucher."

"Hmm. Good point." Maggie returned to his side, barely keeping a straight face. "What do you want me to do, boss? Call the fire department?"

"Are you kidding? Those guys would never let me live this down."

Maggie grinned mischievously. "Speaking of which, this seems like a good time to ask you to promise to call Alison and tell her about the raise you want to give me."

"Are you trying to blackmail me?"

"Now, which television station is it that runs those cute stories about people getting their heads trapped in wrought iron railings and such?"

Robert closed his eyes and sighed. "I called Alison before I left here yesterday and told her what a marvel you were and how I felt your salary should be commensurate with the size of the job here," he informed her impatiently. "Now, would you quit fooling around and hand me that bottle of solvent over there?" he demanded, pointing to a cabinet on the far side of the room.

"Your wish is my command, oh most kind and generous boss man." Maggie bowed dramatically and went to the cabinet. "This bottle?" she asked.

"Damn. It's almost empty," he said with dismay. "There isn't enough there to do any good."

"I can go get some—"

"No! I—I'm getting tired of standing here."

There was more to it than that, Maggie realized. Looking closer, she could see beads of perspiration on his forehead and noticed just a hint of panic in his eyes. Suddenly she understood what his problem was—as well she should, because she suffered from the same malady. She went over to him and put her hand on his shoulder.

"It's all right, Robert," she assured him softly. "We'll get you loose. A few deep breaths always help me when things close in."

Robert looked at her in surprise. "You too?"

"Ever since I was five and my older brother locked me in the hall closet." She looked around the room, grabbed a pair of scissors from a nearby countertop, and held them up with a reassuring smile. "See? We'll just cut your pants off."

"As tempting as that sounds," he replied, staying her hand with his and bobbing his eyebrows roguishly, "these slacks cost me sixty bucks. A little bout of claustrophobia won't hurt me."

Maggie grinned and put down the scissors. "Then you're a better man than I am, Gunga Din. I used to get nauseous just standing still long enough for my mother to mark the hem on my dresses."

"I'm glad I never had to go through that." He looked her up and down, enjoying the tight fit of her jeans and the swell of her full breasts beneath her burgundy-colored blouse. "And might I add that you could never even remotely be mistaken for a man."

"So," she replied, changing the subject and stepping away from him slightly, "what are we going to do?"

Robert looked at the solvent bottle. "Well, let's see how far this takes us." He tipped the bottle up and allowed the remaining drops of liquid to trickle down the front of his pants. Then he tried to pull away from the bench.

"Nothing," Maggie observed.

"No, wait. Something's giving." He pulled again. His zipper started to open. "That's something at least. A little bit farther and I'll be able to get my pants off."

Arching her eyebrows, Maggie said, "Perhaps I should leave while—"

"I need your help," Robert interrupted. "Here. I'll hold the material on either side; you try to shake a few more drops of solvent out while pulling down on the zipper."

"Robert Langley, are you asking me to unzip your pants?"

He met her suspicious gaze. "Will you hurry? This solvent evaporates rapidly," he said seriously. His eyes, however, took on a sensual gleam.

"Robert . . ."

"Ah, come on, Maggie. I've got an ankle-length lab coat on, for heaven's sake!"

He did, but it was unbuttoned. "You planned this whole thing, didn't you?" she asked accusingly. "Stuck yourself to this table just so you could disrobe in front of me."

"As one claustrophobic to another, you know that's not true," he objected. Then he grinned at her. "What's the matter? Are you worried you won't be able to control yourself once you've seen me without my pants on?"

"Ha!"

Glowering at him, she followed his instructions and managed to get the zipper down halfway. His briefs, she couldn't help notice, were the low-cut variety and navy-blue. As he unbuckled his belt and unbuttoned the flap of his slacks, she could also see a line of crisp, very masculine hair disappearing beneath the waistband.

She cleared her throat nervously. "There you go. Now, I really must be getting on with my work," Maggie told him, stepping well away from his muscular body.

"Oh, sure." He looked at her plaintively. "What am I supposed to do? Jump out of these?"

It was clearly impossible. With his pants still stuck to the table by the bottom of the zipper, there was no way he could climb out of them without either ripping them or falling flat on his face.

"All right." She pulled a chair over and put it next to him. "How's that?"

"What good will that do? I can't get my leg up to stand on it."

"Oh." She studied the situation for a moment, then shrugged. "Beats me. You're the creative one."

"Come here."

"Why?" she asked warily.

Robert sighed impatiently. "Just clear this stuff off the table in front of me." She did so. "Now stand on the other side, grab my hands, and help me slide across."

Maggie did as requested, surprised by his smooth skin and strong muscles as he clasped her tightly around the wrists. She pulled and he wiggled his way across the bench, leaving his pants behind. Then he stood up and hugged her.

"We did it! Thanks."

They were laughing, but Maggie was very much aware of his strong thighs pressing against her. His tan, she noticed when the lab coat parted in front, extended to his legs as well. She started to pull away from him, but he held her tight.

"Did you ever wonder," he asked in a soft, teasing voice, "why being held in somebody's arms doesn't make you claustrophobic?"

Looking into his eyes, Maggie didn't feel trapped, exactly, but she did feel impending danger when his lips moved closer to hers. She pulled away again and this time he allowed her to escape.

"I, um, guess I'd better go get some more of that solvent," she said hesitantly.

"Hmm?" Robert murmured distractedly.

"Solvent," she repeated, grabbing the bottle and holding it up. "Unless you want to go get it yourself?"

Robert looked down at his less-than-suitable attire and chuckled. Maggie laughed, too, glad to feel the sensual tension ease between them.

"No," Robert replied, "I think you'd better get it. And hurry," he added, buttoning the lab coat up. "For some reason I'm getting chilly all of a sudden."

* * *

The rest of the morning passed without incident. Lunch was a repeat of yesterday, with Maggie going out and Robert disappearing into his workshop maze with the sandwich she brought back to him.

She was definitely making inroads into the mess. The carpet was actually visible now, and though the desks were still messy underneath, the piles on top were neat and arranged in order of what was to be filed next. Maggie was doing just that, putting files into the cabinets one by one, whistling softly to herself and feeling quite happy with her progress.

"A happy worker is an overpaid worker," Robert commented as he came into the room.

"You can say that after I saved your life this morning?" she asked haughtily.

He laughed. "Well, if not my life, at least a good pair of slacks." He looked around appreciatively. "So that's what the carpet in here looks like."

"You won't recognize the place when I'm through."

Robert watched as she continued her filing, feeling a bit out of place in his own office and not liking it at all. Frowning, he strolled over and poked around on his desk. "I'm already having trouble recognizing it. Where's the Dandy file?" he asked, upset with her for some reason he couldn't put his finger on.

"Right here." She pulled open a drawer in the file cabinet and handed him the folder.

"And the patent documents from the Slippery project?"

Maggie looked at him, puzzled by his angry tone. "That might be a little harder. I'm only up to the *E*'s."

"I've got to have those papers, Maggie. Now."

"Okay, keep your pants on." She laughed at her own joke, but Robert didn't seem to think it was funny. "What's eating you? With the size of the mess around here it's going to take more than two days to get it in order."

Perturbed, he pursed his lips and looked at her for a moment before answering. When he did it was with the tone of a parent scolding an errant child. "Maggie," he began, "I know we need organization around here, and I'm grateful for all the hard work you're doing, but—"

"But what?" she interjected defensively.

"Just because I do things a bit differently sometimes doesn't mean I don't know what I'm doing. When I put papers on my desk I put them there for a reason, and I expect them to stay there until I retrieve them."

"Until you lose them, you mean."

"Now see here, Maggie—"

"No," she shot back, "*you* see here. I don't know what you expect from a temporary worker, but if it's abject obedience you requested the wrong woman. I don't as much work for you as I work for Alison, and that is also a little like being self-employed."

Robert was listening to her with his hands on his hips, surprised by the sudden confrontation but for some reason ready to do battle himself. "Meaning?" he asked.

"Meaning that I'm not shaking in my boots over losing my job. If you terminate my contract, or if I decide I don't want to work here," she added vindictively, wondering why his patronizing tone had gotten her so upset, "with my experience I wouldn't be out of work for more than an hour and a half. You've got leverage? Well, so do I. And if something bothers you about the way I work, by all means let me know, but don't ever use that condescending tone with me again or I'll be out of here so fast it'll make your head spin."

Robert glared at her, angry with himself for having made her mad and with her for looking so damnably attractive when she was furious. "Is that what you want? To quit?"

"No!"

"Well, I don't want you to quit!"

Maggie decided she had never been told she wasn't fired with so much force. Confused, she sat down behind one of the desks and sighed. "Then what was that all about?"

"You're the one who exploded," he said, taking a seat himself and feeling just as confused as she looked.

"Well, excuse me! You're the one who hired me to organize this place and then complained when I started to do it."

"All I said," Robert returned through clenched teeth, "was that there are some things around here that, messy though they may be, are part of the way I operate."

Maggie shook her head. "I don't understand. You agree you need order, right?"

"Right."

"You also agree that having a filing system, a balanced bank account, and the space to actually work in here instead of using it as a storeroom are all good ideas, right?"

Nodding, Robert was suddenly aware he was at a distinct disadvantage. She was expecting him to explain exactly what it was that had irritated him, and he realized he didn't have the slightest idea of what had set him off.

"Right?" Maggie asked again.

Instead of answering her, he started laughing. "That's what I like about you, Maggie." He looked at her lovely, confused face and amended, "Or I should say one of the many things. You're so logical. I find that a very attractive quality."

"One wouldn't think so, judging by the way you jumped on me a moment ago," Maggie replied, standing up and returning to her filing. "I'm only doing my job."

Letting out a long sigh, Robert watched her for a moment, enjoying the easy movements of her body as she worked. At last he stood up and joined her at the filing cabinets.

"I'm sorry," he said sincerely. "I just . . . well,

I've been working alone here for so long and I . . ."

Maggie looked at him and smiled. Robert obviously wasn't used to making apologies. Neither was she, but she made the attempt anyway. "I'm sorry too. I know how it is. You get things just the way you want them—even if it isn't the best way—and it irritates you when someone steps in and starts to change them."

"Yes." He nodded thoughtfully. "It might even go deeper than that with me. Sort of like claustrophobia."

"How's that?" she asked, stopping what she was doing and gazing at him in surprise. "I would have thought that all this clutter would have made it seem like things were closing in on you."

"I suppose it did in a way. But like you said, it was my clutter."

"Sort of a paper security blanket?" Maggie asked with a wide grin.

Robert chuckled. "Whoa. It's getting too near quitting time to have such a philosophical discussion. Suffice it to say that I have this feeling my territory has been invaded."

Looking around at the progress she'd made today, Maggie nodded and gave him a mischievous wink. "It has been invaded. The organization monster has staked her claim."

"Hmm," he murmured, a slight frown wrinkling his brow.

Was that it? Was this working relationship they

were forming making him feel as if Maggie was moving in on him? Why should that bother him? After all, one of the reasons he had hired her was to get closer to her.

Deciding the whole notion was crazy, Robert wiped the frown off his face and shrugged. "Just keep in mind that this is hardly what you'd call an orthodox business, Maggie."

"You can say that again," she said wryly.

"What I mean is, I readily admit I have idiosyncrasies, but that's part of the reason I'm where I am today." He put his nose in the air and added haughtily, "You know. Those flashes of insight, intuitive genius, daring to go where no man has gone before. That sort of thing."

Maggie laughed. "What you are is crazy."

"That too," he agreed.

She gazed at him, realizing that even though he was poking fun at himself there was more than one grain of truth in what he had said. She hadn't just organized his files; out of necessity she had had to read some of them too. He was a very intelligent, creative man. The sheer number of projects he had worked on—not to mention the healthy state of his bank account—proved his success in his chosen profession. Perhaps one did have to be a bit crazy to be an inventor.

"I think I understand what you're saying, Robert," she told him, trying not to sound too serious though she suddenly felt that way. "I'm not here to impinge on your creativity. I'm here to do the job you hired me for, and that is to get the business aspects of your operation into shape. During this transitional phase, I'll try to make things as easy on you as possible, and I promise that when I'm through you won't believe how much smoother things will run for you."

"Transitional phase," Robert repeated, nodding his head appreciatively. "I like that."

She had put her finger on the problem. He was being forced to rely on her more than he had anticipated, but the end result would be in his favor. Order over chaos. Besides, he wasn't about to let his momentary confusion stand in the way of developing a more intimate relationship with Maggie.

"Maybe we can save each other some grief if we mark out our territories," Maggie said, trying to ignore the sudden gleam she saw in his eyes. "The office is mine for now. Until I get things set up, if you need a file I'll get it for you."

"Sounds good," Robert agreed amiably. He barely heard her, lost as he was in a deliciously erotic daydream.

"In return the workshop is yours," she continued. The way he was looking at her made her uneasy, almost as if he was envisioning her without any clothes. "If you want something left alone, carry it into the Stygian depths down there and I'll let it sit as long as it doesn't interfere with what I'm trying to accomplish up here."

Robert roused himself from his mental wanderings and sighed. "Okay. But this territorial thing can't be hard and fast. I'll need to come up and use the phone, do paperwork, and so on." And feast his eyes on her loveliness, he added silently. "Then there's my delinquent logs. In order to get the sequence of events right you'll have to come down and make entries for me while I retrace my steps."

Maggie wasn't sure if she liked that idea. "All right. But if something explodes—"

"I've been working with new formulas for cosmetics for some time now. They don't explode," he assured her, glad she couldn't see that he had his fingers crossed behind his back. "The most you have to worry about is going home smelling a bit odd."

"I suppose I can handle that." She grinned at him, glad they had had this talk. Everything was going to work out just fine. "But keep your glue to yourself. I don't want to end up stuck to a table."

Robert grinned, too, slipping back into his daydreams at the thought of Maggie pinned to a workbench. . . . His grin broadened.

"Robert?" she asked suspiciously as he abruptly turned to leave without answering her. "Where are you going?"

"The Stygian depths."

"But it's quitting time."

"You go on. I have something I have to do first."

"What?"

He chuckled in that evil way that made Maggie's stomach do somersaults. "Hide the bottle of glue solvent," he replied cheerfully. "See you in the morning."

CHAPTER FIVE

"Do you know how long it's been since I've been able to put my feet up on this desk?" Robert asked, doing so with a sigh of contentment. "And have a cup of coffee and a doughnut in the morning without having to excavate a place to sit?"

Maggie walked over to the wastebasket and removed an ancient, half-eaten sweet roll, banging it on the edge of his desk with a *thunk*. "Judging from the sound of this one I found in your drawer, I'd say about a month and a half."

"That wasn't me, that was my sister. She liked to hoard stuff like that."

"Likely story."

They laughed sitting in the office having their morning coffee together. It was Friday, the end of a long, hard week for Maggie, but she felt proud of what she had accomplished thus far. She was a little over halfway through the reorganization of his files, his checkbook was closer to being balanced than it probably ever had been, and yesterday they had even made a start on updating his so-called daily logs.

Best of all, they had gotten through the week without any more arguments. More importantly as far as Maggie was concerned, they had also arrived at the end of the week without any more close encounters of the sensual kind. In fact, Robert had been a perfect gentleman.

She didn't know whether to feel relieved or insulted.

"So," Robert said in a conversational tone, "where shall we go tonight?"

"Go?" she asked, pretending she had forgotten about their date.

"Come on, Maggie. You're not fooling anyone."

True. Not even herself. She was well aware of his anticipation of the evening to come, had noticed the sparkle in his eyes and the spring in his step when he'd come in this morning. Actually, it wasn't his anticipation of the date that had her worried. It was her own. The closer they got to the appointed hour, the more she realized she hadn't looked forward to going out with a man this much in quite some time. Still, she wasn't about to make the mistake of letting him know that.

"Oh. You mean our dinner date," she said at last, acting as if she had just remembered it. "I don't know. Where would you like to go?"

She looked at him, seeing a gleam in his eyes that seemed to indicate he had something other than dinner in mind. But his answer was innocent enough.

"There's a new place I've heard about that's supposed to have the spiciest pan-blackened snapper this side of New Orleans," he replied. "Care to give it a try?"

"Sounds fine." Maybe she was being overly sensitive. Maybe his only plans for this evening were a good dinner and friendly conversation.

And maybe pigs had wings.

"I should tell you, though," Maggie added, "that I'm not much of a night owl. Ten o'clock comes around and I start looking for a place to curl up and read myself to sleep."

Robert grinned. "I'm something of an early-to-bed person myself."

Knowing full well they weren't discussing the same kind of nighttime activity, she still maintained her naive attitude and changed the subject. "Do you work on Saturdays?"

"Sometimes. It depends on what I end up doing on Friday night."

"I see." Did the man ever stop? His subtle innuendos were making her even more nervous about this evening than she already was. "Well, if you need me in the morning, just give me a call."

He chuckled throatily. "I'll do that."

Maggie couldn't take any more. She stood up and began sorting through files. "You know where I'll be if you want me for anything," she said distractedly.

"Am I being dismissed?" he asked. "Thrown from your domain to return to my dungeon?"

"Yes."

Robert laughed, then popped the last of his doughnut into his mouth and swung his long legs off the desk. "You don't need to be so subtle. I know when I'm not wanted." He got to his feet and headed for the door, grabbing one of his log-books on the way out. "See what a good influence you are on me, Maggie? I'm even going to make my entries today as I go along."

"Will wonders never cease?"

"You ain't seen nothin' yet."

"That," Maggie muttered to herself when he had gone, "is precisely what I'm worried about."

Robert climbed the stairs to Maggie's apartment two at a time. He barely noticed the meticulously landscaped yard with its precise squares of green grass and sculpted shrubbery. His mind was on other things.

While at home showering and changing for their date, he had jumped every time the phone rang, fully expecting her to phone and chicken out on him. But she hadn't, and he interpreted it as a promising sign. Perhaps she was looking forward to this evening as much as he was, though probably not for the same reasons.

Full of delicious anticipation and self-confidence, he decided he'd cross that bridge when he came to it and rang the bell, so impatient to see her he felt he'd burst. A frown appeared on his face when she didn't open the door right away. Maybe she was canceling their date by not being at home.

He had just raised his hand to knock when the door opened, revealing a sight that made his breath catch in his throat. Before him stood a very enticing Maggie, fresh from her shower and clad in a white knee-length cotton robe. Her hair was still damp at the edges, fetching little wisps curling around her face. Above the slanted opening of her robe smooth skin greeted his eager gaze. She looked rosy and glowing, good enough to eat. Robert felt his body jump to life at the thought.

"Come on in," she said, standing aside to let him enter. "I'm not quite ready, there—"

"You look fine to me," he interrupted, letting his gaze run the length of her. She had beautiful legs. This wasn't the first time he'd wanted to caress them.

"There was an accident on the highway coming home," Maggie continued as if he hadn't spoken. She closed the door and turned to face him. "Make yourself comfortable. I'll be ready in a few minutes," she said, attempting to slip by him in the narrow hallway without touching him. He made her much too aware she had nothing on beneath the robe.

"Maggie," he said softly, clasping her wrist as she tried to elude him. "I . . ."

"What?" She looked at him over her shoulder, striving to keep the distance between them. His gentle touch on her wrist alone was sending waves of warmth through her.

He ran his thumb over the silky skin of her arm, aware of the rapid beat of her pulse. Patience, he reminded himself, he didn't want to scare her off. "Take your time," he said, letting go of her with great reluctance.

Making a hasty yet dignified retreat, Maggie went to her bedroom, closing the door firmly behind her. She was tempted to collapse on the bed, but was well aware that he'd come looking for her if she didn't appear soon—and bed was the last place she wanted him to find her. Taking a deep breath to calm herself, she started to dress, glad she'd already decided on what to wear.

Robert wandered around the living room enjoying himself. He was discovering another side of Maggie. The walls were cream colored, with two unusual abstract paintings by different artists serving as focal points. Although they could take any form one's imagination desired, he saw a desert after the rain in one, a brewing storm in the other. Somehow he hadn't envisioned her as liking abstract art. She seemed more the realist type, a place for everything and everything in its place.

And he was in for more surprises. Beneath the artwork her sofa came to life with startling splashes of color, the throw pillows picking up where the paintings left off in royal blue, burnt orange, turquoise, and lemon-yellow. The kitchen was typical apartment size, tiny, again with splashes of brilliant color for accent. Her bookcase contained a little of everything, and he was both astounded and pleased to see that there was absolutely no organization in it. Robert shook his head in amazement. Her home spoke of a very different person from the Maggie he knew at work.

He turned around at the sound of the bedroom door opening. "I like your place."

"Thanks," she said, strolling into the room.

He liked what he saw too. A beautiful multicolored print swirled around her legs, showing them off deliciously. Long-sleeved, the dress buttoned from the matching belt up to just above her breasts. A plaited gold chain clung intimately to her neck.

"Definitely worth waiting for," Robert commented appreciatively.

The tingling in her stomach had quieted down while she was dressing, but threatened to start again at his look of desire. Picking up her shawl and evening purse, she walked to the door. "Shall we go?"

"We'd better," he agreed, following her out the door. "I have reservations for this evening."

"You're not the only one," Maggie muttered under her breath.

She enjoyed the drive to the restaurant, though, pleased to find Robert a more conservative driver than she would have thought in view of his sporty Mercedes. The leather upholstery felt good against her legs, quite a change from the vinyl in her own car.

Reservations or not, there was the usual lengthy wait on a Friday night for a table. But the pair were finally seated and found the service good and the food excellent. The dining room was bathed in a soft pink glow of light, each booth and table equipped with an antique lamp which was adjustable to the desired level of intimacy.

"Tell me about getting started," Maggie suggested as they relaxed over coffee and dessert.

"I'd rather talk about you."

"You promised," she reminded him, savoring the creamy texture of her peanut butter cheesecake drizzled in rich chocolate sauce. It was surprisingly light, airy, and nothing short of heavenly.

Robert was in a different kind of heaven. He watched her take another bite, her eyes almost closing as she tasted the dessert. The tip of her tongue darted out to flick back an errant crumb, making him wish he were that crumb.

"Well?" she prompted. It was obvious he didn't want to talk about himself, but she was determined.

Robert shrugged. "What do you want to know?" He recognized that look in her eyes. She could be just as tenacious as she was lovely.

"Everything."

She sat back, glad for the low lighting as she ran her eyes over him. He looked good this evening, his camel hair jacket, crisp white shirt, and striped tie enhancing his personality. He was a very unusual man. A very attractive man. She took a sip of her liqueur-laced coffee to calm a sudden attack of nerves. It helped.

"Okay, I was born on—"

"I already know that," she inserted. "Let's skip ahead a few years."

Robert arched his eyebrows. "What do you mean you already know? How'd you find that out?"

"Your files tell everything." She paused, then added slyly, "Providing one is smart enough to find all the pieces." Smiling at him innocently, she continued. "Let's start with your first experiment."

"Vinegar and baking soda, naturally," he replied. "Isn't that where every kid starts out?" Looking at her speculatively, he added, "But then I suppose you were probably too concerned with making a mess even at that age, right?"

"I'll have you know I made some superlative messes at that age," she informed him. "And yes, I fiddled with soda and vinegar too. Smelly foam all over the kitchen. The only difference was that unlike some people I know, I cleaned up after myself."

Robert shrugged, refusing to rise to the bait. "Anyway, I got my first beginners' chemistry set when I was twelve," he continued, putting down his coffee cup. He looked up at her and smiled in remembrance. "I was hooked. The local library was never safe from me again."

"What do you mean?"

"I used to check out books, put together pieces of different experiments, and then stand back to see what would happen." He chuckled at the memories.

"Knowing you, you probably blew up the books."

"Close. In the beginning I only covered them in whatever glop I was experimenting with." He looked up to find her listening intently. "But I quickly learned to put the books in drawers or cover them."

"A sense of academic responsibility at such an early age? I'm impressed."

"Don't be," he replied, pausing to take a bite of his cheesecake and finding the unusual taste quite good. "It was more like a sense of financial responsibility, and it was all my mother's doing."

This was more like it. Tales from his formative years. "What did she do?" Maggie asked, finding the twinkle in his gray eyes quite appealing as he spoke.

"Made me pay for the ruined books out of my nonexistent allowance."

Maggie had a good hunch about what his mother had really done to control a boy who had undoubtedly been a tough one to handle. "In other words she made you work it off, right?"

"Better her than my dad. She gave me at least twice the amount of money for the same chore."

That was easy to believe. He had probably had

winning ways with women even then. "How about your first invention?"

"You don't want to know."

"I really do," she told him earnestly.

Robert shook his head. "You really don't. You know how boys are at that age," he informed her cryptically. "Preoccupied with the female of the species."

"What on earth . . ." Maggie's voice trailed off. She was intrigued, but decided he was right. The mind of a frustrated teenage boy was not something she really wanted to delve into.

"Of course," he continued, laughing at the confused expression on Maggie's face, "some of us never outgrow that particular preoccupation. Sex is one area of knowledge I will never tire of exploring." He reached across the table and put his hand on top of hers.

"I'll bet," she returned dryly, pulling free of his grasp and holding her coffee cup with both hands. "You seem quite intent on continuing your education."

"I am." He grinned wickedly. "Very intent."

Maggie couldn't believe it. Here she was, trading double entendres with her boss! She had to get this conversation back on a more suitable track.

"I just thought of something," she said, though in fact it was a question she'd been meaning to ask him. "I didn't see any of your diplomas while I was sorting through the office. Do you keep them at home?"

"Them?" Robert seemed to find her question immensely amusing. "You make it sound as if every college in America tried to recruit me out of high school or something."

In view of his intelligence and success, that was precisely what she thought. "I assumed they did."

"In truth I barely made it out of high school," he explained. "I managed to get tossed out of a couple of junior colleges as well. I'm afraid I was too involved with trying to invent something new all the time to pay much attention to my studies."

"Did your parents mind?"

He laughed. "Mind? They were thankful I managed to get as much formal education as I did without being expelled." He paused as the waiter freshened their coffee. "Actually, I'm glad I struck out on my own."

"Why?"

"If I'd stayed in school, I might not have accomplished as much as I have. You see, I don't know any better. I don't have my head crammed with all these scientific reasons why I can't do something," Robert explained seriously. "It's enabled me to find solutions to problems by looking in directions other people wouldn't consider because they've been taught the answers can't be found that way."

"Ignorance is bliss?" Maggie asked doubtfully.

"Not ignorance, exactly," he replied. "I guess you'd call it selective forgetfulness. I was actually pretty sharp in school, started out at the top of my class in physics, chemistry, and math."

"What went wrong?"

"Too many chemistry experiments went wrong. I became more interested in finding the limits of whatever it was I was doing than I was in completing the assignment." He grinned contritely. "And of course the rest of the class liked my way better. I was the leader and considered the most dangerous."

Her eyes widened in mock surprise. "Imagine that!"

"Hey! I haven't blown up anything since you've been working for me, have I?"

"No, just glued yourself to a table," she reminded him. "And it's only been a week. I figure you're waiting until I get most of the mess in the office taken care of before you give way with any little surprises." She sipped her coffee, grinning at him as he took on an offended air. "Forget it," she advised. "I remember why your last employee left."

"Faint of heart."

"Probably wanted to keep her heart a few more years," she retorted dryly. "Anyway, getting back to your high school exploits . . ."

"Do you really want to know?" he asked skeptically. "Or are you just fishing for more ammunition to get yourself that hazardous duty pay?"

She shook her head at him. "Cut the stalling tactics and give."

"What would you like?" He slipped his hand across the table to possess hers, grasping her more firmly this time so she couldn't pull away without making a scene.

"High school remembrances," she reminded him, trying to ignore the tingling sensations running up her arm. "I'm trying to figure out what kind of man I've gotten myself involved with."

She regretted her choice of words immediately, but Robert didn't pursue her slip of the tongue. He simply smiled, the now-familiar sensual gleam returning to his eyes.

He sighed dramatically. "I suppose the beginning of the end of my academic career came during my senior year. My lab partner and I were working after school, trying out this idea we had for a complexion cream. We were sure it would win us the undying appreciation of every woman in the world." He looked at her and winked. "If you know what I mean."

Maggie chuckled, the warmth of his hand on hers doing unusual things to her metabolism. "I'm getting a pretty good idea of how your mind works, yes."

"Our teacher walked in on us and," Robert paused, a thoughtful expression on his face. "To this day I don't know what went wrong."

"It didn't!"

He rolled his eyes. "It did. There was this massive, um, eruption, I suppose you'd call it. The stuff went all over her, barely touched us."

"And she was not amused, I take it?"

"Three-day suspension. Avoided us like the plague for the rest of the year," he admitted. "Not to mention tearing up my notes. Darn shame too. I still maintain her skin never looked better—once she managed to scrape the stuff off, that is. But without knowing just what or how much we had put into the brew . . ."

Maggie shook her head, laughing, while Robert seemed to drift off into another world for a moment. He was not so far gone, however, that he forgot he was holding her hand. He caressed her palm with his thumb, drawing tiny circles on the silky soft skin.

"What happened next?" she asked, trying to break him from his reverie. His finger was slipping under the cuff of her sleeve, stroking her arm suggestively.

"Hmm?" He looked up at her. "Oh. I decided to start working with mechanical things." He grinned at her roguishly. "Things that didn't blow up."

She moved her hand back, free from his devilishly exciting touch. These tales of his inventive exploits had her more at ease with him than she had thought possible. Too much at ease. She reminded herself to watch her step.

"Somehow, I doubt the change to mechanics was your choice. Am I right?"

"Yes. It was shop class or home economics, and the home economics teacher pleaded with my parents to spare her a fate worse than death. But I enjoyed learning about mechanical devices just as much, if not more."

"Automatic window blinds, doors that open with credit cards. I'm surprised you don't have entry by palm print or something."

He sighed. "Too late. The government's had those for years, I'm afraid. I'm working on an improvement, though," he said, then looked at her speculatively, struck with the uneasy feeling she already knew. He wondered if he'd left any more files he didn't want anyone to know about carelessly out in the open.

"I saw those in a movie once," she said, not noticing his suspicious gaze. "I think it would be great not to have to carry all those keys around." She looked at the palm of her hand, frowning slightly. "How does it work?"

"You tell me."

Maggie looked at him, confused by his odd tone of voice. "Excuse me?"

"Nothing," he muttered, deciding he was just having a sudden fit of inventor's paranoia. Replacing his frown with a smile, he paid the bill, then took her hand again and stood up. "I think we'd better leave before the restaurant manager starts charging us rent."

"I suppose you're right." She stood up, too, and they strolled out to the parking lot. When they got to his car it was Maggie's turn to frown uncertainly. "Where should we go?" she asked, surprised to find herself unwilling to end this date just yet.

Robert's smile grew broader. "Oh, we'll think of something."

CHAPTER SIX

"This is sweet of you, Robert," Maggie said when he pulled up in front of her apartment, "but I was exaggerating when I said I fall asleep at ten o'clock."

"Great!" he exclaimed happily. "Then you won't mind if I come up. We can talk some more."

Maggie turned to look at him, reasonably certain she had just been had. "That wasn't what I meant, Robert. I—"

"Of course," he interrupted, "we could always go dancing or something. I know this quiet, intimate little place not far from here."

She didn't like the way he had said *intimate*. The thought of having him in her apartment suddenly seemed much safer than dancing cheek to cheek in some dimly lighted lounge with romantic music playing softly in the background. His powerful masculine aura was much too tempting. At least here, in her own home, if worst came to worst she could lock herself in her bedroom.

"My, my," she replied, faking a yawn. "I think I could use another cup of coffee, couldn't you?"

"My thought exactly," Robert agreed, well aware of her ploy and doing his best not to grin. She'd walked right into his trap just as he knew she would. "Shall we?" he asked, bounding out of the car before she could reply and suggest a coffee shop.

"Oh, what the heck," Maggie muttered, taking his hand when he came around to her side and opened the door. "But it will have to be tea. I just remembered I didn't have time to go to the store on my way home."

"I love tea."

"Naturally."

Robert followed her up the stairs to her apartment, watching the gentle sway of her hips as she took each step. He stood close to her, feeling the heat of her body, waiting patiently for her to find the right key.

"I don't suppose you could put one of those credit card locks on my door, could you?" Maggie grumbled, fumbling with her overloaded key ring.

"Sure. I have one left over from a batch I installed at my house." He grinned slyly. "Your door would have the same code as mine. Wouldn't that be nice?"

"On second thought, never mind." She found the key and tried to put it in the lock, irritated by the sudden trembling of her hand. "Darn."

Robert reached around her to help, using it as

an excuse to enclose her in his embrace. "May I?" he asked, placing his hand on hers.

"It sticks sometimes," she explained, trying to ignore the feel of his hair whispering along her throat as he bent to fiddle with the lock.

"You should call maintenance to fix this." Finally he got the balky mechanism to work. "Not that I mind helping you one bit," he murmured, kissing the vulnerable area behind her ear.

Maggie shivered and pulled away from him, flipping on a light to dispel the intimacy of the moment. He followed her inside, locking the door behind him and loosening his tie. Then he removed it and unbuttoned his collar, all the while smiling at her innocently.

"Make yourself comfortable," she said dryly as he dropped his tie on the couch.

"Thanks. I will." He unbuttoned two more buttons of his shirt, slipped his jacket off, and breathed a sigh of relief.

She cursed herself for making the suggestion even in jest. He looked too sexy in the white dress shirt, his golden tan showing where he had unbuttoned the collar. What had she been thinking of when she'd invited him up? Maybe a dance floor would have been safer after all, with other people around to keep things from getting out of hand.

"Relax, Maggie." He picked up a royal blue pillow from the couch and put it aside, then settled himself comfortably on the soft cushions, looking curiously at the way she stood frozen on the other side of the room. "I'm not going to pounce on you." He paused, then added, "Tonight."

She tried to ignore the implied promise of things to come. Turning, she walked into the kitchen and opened a cupboard, smiling to herself. Perhaps she was saved after all.

"Looks like I'm out of tea as well. Sorry."

"I saw some brandy on your kitchen counter earlier. A drop or two of that would be nice."

Maggie sighed. He was an observant devil. Resigning herself to the fact that Robert was determined to stay for a while, she got down her brandy snifters, knowing she didn't need this added provocation to her senses. Her body was already stimulated enough; his soft touch and subtle sensuality had seen to that. She jumped when he spoke from the doorway, his unexpected presence making her heart race.

"Need any help?"

Maggie shook her head and picked up the glasses, handing him one. He stood in the middle of the small kitchen, making it impossible for her to slip past without brushing against him. Cornered. She felt trapped and decided to let him know it.

"Kind of close quarters in here," she said.

"I think it's cozy." He hesitated for a moment, just looking at her, then returned to the couch. More unsure of herself than ever, she followed.

"Have a seat," Robert offered. Piling the pillows in the middle of the couch, he cleared a spot for her. He chuckled when she hesitated, seeing her eyes dart to a chair far away from him on the other side of the room. "Afraid?" he taunted softly.

Maggie straightened, determined to put up a brave front. "Of course not." She sat down on the other side of his pile of pillows with a regal air, nonchalantly taking a sip of her brandy. The potent liquid blazed a path of smooth fire all the way down her throat, giving her added courage. Still, she carefully avoided looking at him.

He glanced at her as he took one of the pillows between them and put it out of the way on the coffee table with measured deliberation. "I like your taste in artwork," he said, looking at the paintings.

"Thank you."

What was she so worried about? This was her house, he was her boss, and he knew her feelings about getting involved with him. She had to show him she wasn't the slightest bit uneasy. Kicking off her high heels, she curled her legs up beside her and smoothed the silky material of her dress over them.

"My brothers gave me that one," she said, pointing out the painting. "I bought the other with my last bonus."

"Brothers?" She had only mentioned one, older and with a penchant for locking her in closets.

"Two. One older and one younger." She leaned back against the corner of the sofa, relaxing as she thought of her family. "George is twenty-two, has one year of college left. Harry's twenty-eight, an engineer, working over in Australia right now."

"Oh," Robert hummed, interested but distracted at the moment by the lovely view of her legs her position afforded him. "Australia you say?" He casually removed another pillow from the barrier between them.

Maggie nodded, aware of his hungry gaze and the way he was moving closer to her, but determined not to appear concerned. "Quite fond of the place, according to his letters," she replied. "Personally, though, I think what he's really fond of are the attire-optional beaches."

"I like the sound of that myself. What do you say we hop on the next flight and do some sun worshiping together?" He moved another pillow out of the way. "I have a feeling you look great wearing just your tan."

"Oh, you do, do you?" she asked, shocked by the husky sound of her own voice. It must be the brandy, she decided.

He reached out and took hold of her glass, putting both of them on the table. "Is that an invitation?" he murmured, dislodging the rest of the pillows onto the floor as he slipped beside her. "Or a dare?"

"Neither. Robert, I . . ."

"Yes?" he whispered, pulling her into his arms and sinking back on the couch.

Maggie flowed with him. She was vibrantly aware that every inch of her body touched his.

Their hips were pressed intimately together, the hardness of his thighs branding his imprint upon her softness. The muscles of her calves quivered, contracting at his touch as his hands glided over her smooth skin. But he seemed to be leaving the choice up to her; she could get up and walk away if she wanted to. So why didn't she?

"Don't you want to kiss me?" he asked, clasping his arms loosely around her waist.

She looked down at him, uncertain about what she really did want. He was hard, masculine, yet not demanding or overbearing. And the thought of kissing him again was very, very tempting. Maybe just one.

Moving her hands to either side of his head, she lowered her mouth to his, brushing her lips against his. To her great surprise he didn't respond, didn't grab her and kiss her back. She pulled away from him slightly, confused by his closed eyes and expressionless face. What was this? A challenge?

Maggie chuckled then, catching on to his game. Maybe it was the brandy, or the pleasant dinner and conversation they had shared, but she was suddenly less concerned with the fact that she worked for him. What she wanted to do right now was surprise him, show him that two could play at this teasing contest.

"You asked for it," she told him throatily. Leaning closer, she flicked his lips with her tongue, gauging his response. When barely a movement showed, her eyes widened in outrage. "Why, you!"

She ran her fingers through his thick brown hair before undoing the next button on his shirt. She slid her hand over the cloth and inside to cover his heart. His racing pulse pleased her immensely. She leaned close to him again and whispered in his ear.

"Gotcha!"

"No, I've got you," he said, wrapping his arms tightly around her.

"Hey!" she cried, trying to pull away.

"Such a little tease."

"You asked for it."

"That's not all I asked for. Please keep struggling," he ordered, looking down the front of her dress. The top two buttons had opened, revealing her lacy bra.

"Stop that, you—"

He cut her off, covering her mouth with his. He tasted of warm brandy, intoxicating and arousing. She had teased him and she knew it, causing their game to turn serious. Maggie didn't know what payment he planned to demand for her teasing, but what really had her worried was that she suddenly didn't care. Their tongues mingled with desire and she was reveling in every moment.

Breathing heavily, he rolled onto his side, bringing her with him. "Were you thinking of me when you dressed this evening?" he murmured. Deftly he opened the front clasp of her bra, revealing her breasts to his gaze.

"Robert!" She turned her head as a delicate pink

blush cascaded down from her face to the delicate skin of her throat.

"Shh, I only want to feel you against me." Baring his chest, he touched her warm skin to his. The tips of her breasts seemed to singe his already heated flesh.

"I'm not ready for this." But her objection was more a moan of pleasure as she fought with her own emotions.

"We won't go any further than you want," he murmured.

"I . . ." She moaned again as he pulled her even tighter against his broad chest, flattening her breasts against his hardness.

"Just a taste," he whispered.

Bending his head down, he enclosed one rosy tip between his lips. His tongue laved it with attention before sliding over to its twin. One hand slipped up under her dress, caressing her thighs, the patience he had vowed to maintain with her fast disappearing. He traced the shape of her legs before gliding his hand around and over her buttocks, then up to her trim waist. His errant, daring hand slid inside her pantyhose to feel her silky skin as he held her intimately against him.

She could feel his hard masculinity pressing firmly against her. Coils of desire were spiraling through her body, twisting and turning as they wove a blanket of fire around her. He felt so good, his hands upon her like a cooling balm to the flames of her desire, yet at the same time spreading still more heat wherever he touched. She had to tell him before she lost complete control.

"Robert, listen to me," she said, pulling away from his body, trying desperately to force her passion-clouded mind to function.

"I'm listening. I can even hear your heart beating, feel it beneath my hand." He continued to caress her, his eyes closed in bliss.

"Open your eyes."

"Gladly." He complied, his eyes continuing where his hands had stopped. Desire burned in his eyes when he saw how flushed her skin had become.

"I'm not ready for this. And not only that, I'm not prepared either," she told him, blurting out the words.

His head dropped back over the edge of the sofa as her meaning finally penetrated his brain. "Oh, Lord, I hadn't even thought of that."

"We have to stop."

"Damn." He sighed, rolled over in frustration, and promptly fell off the couch.

"Robert! Are you okay?" she asked, leaning on her elbow and looking down at him.

He lay sprawled on her bright pillows, the words coming out of his mouth colorful enough to match his impromptu bed. A laugh escaped Maggie before she could suppress it.

"Think it's funny, do you?" he asked, grasping her wrist. "Then come on down." He yanked on her arm and she came sprawling down on top of him.

"Oof! You, sir, are not a soft landing."

"You're no lightweight yourself, ma'am," he muttered, shifting her off his most vulnerable area.

"Did I hurt you?"

"Nothing that won't mend." A sensuous gleam flashed into his eyes. "Would you like to kiss it better?"

"Feels better to me already," she retorted.

"A little extra help never hurt."

"After that remark about my weight, you'd chance my wrath?" she asked, jabbing him in the ribs. "Not to mention my teeth."

His eyes widened. "You really know how to put a crimp in a guy's fantasies, don't you?" He tried to evade her jabs and ended up hitting his shoulder on the coffee table. "This place is booby-trapped!" he exclaimed in defeat, flopping back on the floor.

"Only to those who deserve it," she taunted.

"I didn't mean anything by my comment. Your figure is great." He combed his fingers through her shiny brown hair, then slid it behind her ears, yanking on it gently. "At least what I've seen so far."

She could feel it starting again, that longing inside her that seemed bent on making a mockery of her willpower and intelligence. This was insane!

Maggie rolled under the narrow coffee table and out of his grasp. "That's all you're going to see tonight!" What had gotten into her? Straightening her clothes, she picked up her brandy and took a big gulp.

Robert watched the emotions breezing across her face, trying to interpret them. He didn't know or understand Maggie, but he intended to. He had seen and felt her fire, and he wouldn't rest until he convinced her to let the flames consume her.

"You serve one heck of a nightcap," he said, grinning as he stood up and sipped the last of his brandy.

"Button your shirt," she ordered, turning her back on him. That smooth expanse of tanned chest and hard muscle of his would be her undoing.

He finished his drink and walked toward her, trying to gauge her feelings by her stance. "I'd like to see you again, Maggie."

Maggie turned on him, her uncertainty clearly visible on her face. "You're my boss. Of course you'll see me again."

"You know what I mean." He was standing within inches of her, but did not touch her. "And you also know perfectly well that what's happening between us has little to do with who's in charge. You're a consummate secretary, but if that's all I was interested in I could find one who wasn't so insubordinate."

"You—you—"

"And even that doesn't stop me from wanting you."

"I won't allow it!"

112

He cradled her face in his hands. "And I'm just as determined to change your mind."

His kiss was soft and sweet, his lips brushing hers gently, evoking a longing in her she didn't think she even wanted to control. He released her slowly, stepping back to button up his shirt and slip on his jacket.

"See you Monday," he said, sliding one finger down her cheek before walking out the door.

Maggie closed and locked it behind him, then collapsed into the nearest chair, her emotions so haywire she didn't know what she was thinking anymore.

He spelled trouble, that was for sure. She had always prided herself on her common sense, but when Robert touched her it all flew with the wind. Like it or not, she was in for the ride of a lifetime, and she wasn't at all sure who was at the controls.

"Up, up, and away," she muttered under her breath.

CHAPTER SEVEN

"Inventors," Maggie groaned in despair, covering her head with her pillow. "Ugh! I hate you, Alexander Graham Bell."

It was no use. Her phone kept ringing, and ringing, forcing her eyes open in spite of her best efforts to keep them closed. Who could be so rude? Wasn't it obvious she wasn't home? She was in just the right mood to tell whoever it was exactly what she thought of their manners.

After Robert left last night she'd started a new book to take her mind off what had happened between them. The story, full of mystery and intrigue, had been good enough to make for an almost sleepless night.

It had also turned out to be exactly what Maggie didn't need—a plot woven around a romance so steamy she hadn't been able to put the book down until two in the morning. Even then the scintillating exploits of the hero and heroine had kept her imagination running overtime.

"All right. I give up." She threw the pillow to

the floor and crawled out of bed, grumbling dire threats. "Wait till I find that phone. Whoever you are, you're going to get an earful," she promised vindictively. Following the obnoxious ring, she shuffled into the living room, grabbed the receiver, and answered in a curt tone.

"Yes?" Total silence. Not even heavy breathing. "Is anyone there?" she yelled. How dare they hang up after getting her out of bed!

"Maggie, is that you?"

Robert. Naturally. Who else would be insensitive enough to let the phone ring forty times? She picked up the rest of the phone and walked into the kitchen, giving him a taste of his own medicine by not saying a word.

"Maggie, are you there?" he asked, louder this time.

The temptation to hang up on him was strong, but she wrote the urge off as childish. "Yes."

"I was beginning to think you weren't home." Relief was evident in his voice.

"Whatever gave you that idea?" she asked sarcastically, opening the nearest cupboard and peering inside.

"Listen, I'm going to take you up on your offer."

Maggie jerked the next cupboard open as if trying to take the contents by surprise. It didn't work. "What offer?" she asked suspiciously. Maybe the freezer. Crossing her fingers, she stepped over to it and slowly opened the door. Nothing.

"To come into work today. I need some information from the files, and, well . . . I can't find anything."

"Poor baby." She had to face the facts: She really was out of coffee. "Did you mess with my files?" she asked, her mind drifting back to their conversation.

Her mild tone of voice didn't fool him. "Only one," he lied. "Can you come in and deal with this mess?"

"Mess?" she inquired cautiously. "What mess?"

Robert cleared his throat. "I mean the monster filing system you created. It's Greek to me."

"If you misplaced so much as one of those files, I'll—"

He interrupted her before she could really get going. "How soon can you get here?"

Maggie wandered back into her bedroom and sat on the bed. A ray of hope entered her foggy mind. "Do you have coffee ready?"

"Yes." He decided to use his secret weapon. "With a fresh almond pastry," he told her, his voice smooth and coaxing.

"I'll be in soon," she said, hanging up on him. If she didn't watch out she'd be gaining weight on this job.

The tantalizing scent of fresh brewed coffee hit Maggie the moment she entered the warehouse, an invisible vapor lifting her up the stairs like a character in a cartoon. There it was, liquid salvation, a full pot waiting just for her, and beside it the added temptation of the promised almond pastry.

"Hello, you lovely little rascals," she cooed.

By the time she was starting her second cup, Maggie decided she might make it through the day after all. Even straightening up the files Robert had managed to strew everywhere didn't faze her. Then she jumped right in and continued with yesterday's project.

For a man in such a hurry to see her earlier, Robert was certainly taking his own sweet time coming up to the office. Maggie wasn't about to go looking for him. She was worried about how he would behave after last night. In fact, she didn't know how *she* would react at seeing him this morning, and decided to put off their meeting for as long as possible. Maybe he had found what he needed and she wouldn't see him at all.

No such luck. She heard the sound of footsteps on the stairs. "Speak of the devil," she muttered.

He came sailing into the office and headed straight for the coffee. "Maggie, could you find me the information on the Trescott project, please?"

Carefully putting the file on her desk well out of his reach, she started looking for the one he wanted. "Trescott," she mumbled to herself. With so many new files she could be wrong, but she couldn't remember one by that name.

Robert watched her going through the stacks of papers, feeling a grudging admiration for her efficiency. He couldn't find a thing in this maze of

117

organization and was prepared to be properly impressed if she could. He was already quite impressed with the way her jeans molded to her curves. Of course, the lemon-yellow sweatshirt she was wearing hid most of her upper body, but he had a good memory for some things.

"What's in the file?"

He thought about the file in question. "Not much. A few notes to myself, some basic formulae. It's a project I'm about to start on," he answered distractedly. Loose as it was, he could still see a nice outline of her breasts beneath her top. He smiled.

She looked at him suspiciously, crossing her arms over her chest in a self-conscious gesture. Only he could find something sexy about her deliberately concealing attire. "When you called, you made it sound as if you needed a file to *finish* a project," she accused. "Not some vague outline of one that could have waited until Monday."

"I do. But since you're here I'm hoping you can find this other one for me too," he replied smoothly.

Maggie gave him an assessing look. What was he up to this time? He appeared to be acting like a few other male employers she'd known—roving eyes but all business. Maybe he had thought it over and decided she was right about their relationship. She hoped so, because whether he liked it or not, that was exactly the way she expected things to be: Look but don't touch.

118

"You'll have to give me more information on that file if you expect me to find it. I don't even remember one by that name, which means it's probably still buried somewhere," she informed him. She was expecting him to rant and rave or at least say I told you so, but he didn't.

"It's not important." He glanced briefly at her, then cut another slice of pastry. "Have you found any more of the Slippery project?"

Maggie walked over to his desk. "Right where you can't miss it." She held up a file.

"And the last place I'd look." He took the papers from her and bopped her on the head with them. "You did that on purpose."

Maggie grinned at him and returned serenely to her desk. It was true. He had accepted her wish to keep things professional, at least at the office. "Do you need anything else, sir?" she inquired in her best secretarial voice.

It was tempting to tell her exactly what he needed from her, but he replied, "Not right now."

She sat erect, her feet flat on the floor, fingers intertwined and resting gently on the desk. The signals coming from her were loud and clear. He intended to respect her wishes at the moment—in his own special way, naturally.

"If you have any needs," he added, his gray eyes twinkling, "or questions, please feel free to come downstairs."

She pursed her lips as he turned on his heel and left the room. Then she shrugged. He could look and he could talk, just as long as he kept those deliciously experienced hands to himself.

Maggie had just started down the stairs when she noticed an odd smell emanating from the workshop. Pleasantly sweet, almost perfumelike, it wasn't a disagreeable odor at all, but it did make her pause for a moment and wonder whether to continue on or run back to the safety of the office. Still, she wanted to ask Robert what he'd like for lunch, so she screwed up her courage and entered his domain.

He was working in his chemistry lab, standing at a worktable covered with all sorts of bubbling, steaming beakers of some milky white substance. He was standing so still Maggie's first thought was that he had glued himself to the table again. Then she realized he was concentrating intently on the passage of the white stuff through some sort of glass spiral. It went around and around the tube, then dripped through a nozzle into a dish underneath.

The process was hypnotic in a way. The stuff in the beaker would bubble, steam would rise, then around and through the apparatus it would go, like a little white mouse running a maze, finally dripping with a thick plop into the waiting dish.

"What on earth is that stuff?" she asked, warily stepping closer for a better look.

"Shh!"

"Excuse me!" Maggie returned in a wounded

tone. "I was just coming to see if you wanted lunch."

"Uh-huh," Robert mumbled.

"Is that a yes or a no?"

He shook his head in annoyance, simultaneously making adjustments to the flame of the gas burner and a valve on the condensing tube. "Maggie, please!"

"This is the thanks I get for trying to see to it you don't starve."

Robert sighed and turned around. "This is a tricky procedure. Would you please—" He stopped midsentence and touched the back of his head, a startled expression on his face. His eyes widened. "Oh, no! Not again!"

"What do you . . ."

The first thing Maggie noticed was that Robert's hair was turning white. Then she felt something warm all over her face. A hissing noise filled her ears, echoing off the walls of the lab and the warehouse ceiling high above their heads. She heard a loud pop.

And then it started to snow.

But it wasn't snow. It was rain, milky white, warm, and sticky as whatever Robert had been cooking up sprayed from a hole in the apparatus. It covered the walls, the floor, the cabinets, and the tables, but most of all it covered the two shocked people standing nearest the flow. Misty fine at first, it gradually changed to thick globs that flew across the room, landing with disgusting splats on anything in its path.

Finally, as quickly as it had begun, the eruption stopped. With the hissing sound gone, they could hear the white substance dripping from every surface. Other than that there was total silence.

Maggie looked around in disbelief. There was some kind of creamy white stuff all over her. It was in her hair, all over her shirt and jeans, and even her tennis shoes had a few globs on them. Robert hadn't fared much better. He had his lab coat on, but it was saturated. He was covered with the goo from head to toe, rivulets the consistency of sour cream running down his face.

"Robert," Maggie said through clenched teeth, afraid to open her mouth, "I am going to kill you."

He reached to clean off her face. "Here, let me—"

"Don't touch me!" she cried.

"Oh." Looking at his hands, he realized touching her would only put more of the stuff on her. As the one closest to the leak, he had borne most of its wrath. He looked again at the outrage and disgust on Maggie's face and started to laugh. "You should see yourself!"

"You planned this!" she exclaimed in outrage, taking a menacing step toward him.

"Don't be silly. I couldn't possibly . . ."

Maggie ran her hands down the front of her sweatshirt, scooping up as much of the glop as she could hold, then she shook her hands at him and watched with satisfaction as it splattered all over his face.

"Thanks a bunch."

"What is this stuff?" she asked, looking at herself again and feeling on the verge of tears.

"Complexion cream. Don't worry, it's non-toxic," he assured her. "As a matter of fact, it's good for you." He reached out and patted her cheeks with both hands, his touch making a sound like someone playing in wet cement. "Here, have some more."

"Ugh! It doesn't feel like any complexion cream I've ever used." She grimaced and backed away from him.

"Of course not. It's a special formula I'm working on." He tried to rub it into his hands, but there was way too much of the stuff. He gazed at Maggie, an evil gleam in his eyes. "It would be a shame to waste it. Let's share."

"Robert . . ."

He lunged for her, grabbing her wrists. "How would you like this all over you?" he whispered sensuously.

"W-what do you mean?" she stuttered, the slippery feel of his hands on hers arousing her senses.

"You know what I mean." Robert pulled her close, sliding his hands up under her top to caress her bare midriff. She shuddered beneath his touch and he smiled. "It'll make your skin so smooth and soft. Doesn't that feel good?"

"No!" But it did. It felt very good, and after last

night her emotions were already honed to a fevered pitch. "Stop that!" she pleaded, her voice sounding throaty and breathless even to her.

"Relax," he whispered. "I'll give you an allover beauty treatment."

Maggie moaned as his fingers spread open across her rib cage and drew slippery, sensuous patterns on her skin. Then he was stroking her back, one finger sliding up and down her spine, evoking tingling sensations all the way to her toes.

"We're supposed to be sharing," he reminded her in a teasing voice. "Touch me."

Her mind swimming with pleasure as his wandering hands caressed her sides, she reached out to unbutton his shirt, wanting to touch him as intimately as he was touching her. But she managed to stop herself just in time. Nothing had changed from last night.

"I can't!"

"You want to," he encouraged.

"We're at work, Robert," she objected, grabbing at straws to interrupt his sensual play.

His deft fingers had found the catch to her bra, but were so slippery he couldn't quite get it open. The heat of his body so close to hers was playing havoc with her resolve.

"This is a security building, remember? Nobody has access but you and me." He finally freed her breasts from their lacy prison. "And this time," he added, nibbling on her neck, "I'm prepared."

His hands glided over the swelling globes of her

124

breasts, the slick feel of his palms on her nipples making her feel weak in the knees. What argument could she use now? Nothing came to mind, and she realized there wasn't one that would make him stop this sensual assault. Not only that, she didn't want him to stop. The fire coursing through her could be extinguished in only one way.

"Robert . . ." Her voice trailed off in a moan as he gently stroked the hard tip of each breast with his thumbs. She had to give it one last try. "Please . . ."

Much to her surprise he seemed to heed her breathless plea. His caresses stopped, making her open her eyes and look at him questioningly. He looked puzzled too.

"What the . . ." A frown furrowed his goo-covered brow. "Oh, Lord."

"What!" Maggie yelped.

"This stuff," he said as he pulled his hands from under her shirt, "seems to be getting thicker."

Feeling frustrated and angry, Maggie tried to point an accusing finger at him, but found them all stuck together. "I knew it! You've glued us to death!"

He laughed and put his arms around her, patting her back sympathetically. "It's not that bad," he assured her. Then he noticed he had trouble pulling away from her. "On second thought . . . come on. If I'm going to be stuck to you for life, I don't want it to be with all my clothes on."

"Get away from me!" Maggie yelled, practically in hysterics as she tried to push him away.

But Robert kept pulling her by the hand, leading her at a run through the maze of workshops, back into the depths of the warehouse to a spot she hadn't known was there. It appeared to be some kind of studio apartment, complete with kitchenette and sleeping quarters, but Maggie had little time to look it over even if she had had the inclination. Robert was pulling her into a surprisingly large, well-equipped bathroom.

"What is this place?"

"My home away from home. I had it built after one too many nights of sleeping on my workshop tables."

Maggie headed straight for a large mirror over the sink and surveyed the damage. Trying not to look too closely at herself, she pushed her dripping, white-streaked brown hair out of the way and began gently wiping her face with a tissue. To her surprise her makeup came right off along with the cream, and she also noticed the stuff had left her skin feeling incredibly soft.

"Great makeup remover," she quipped.

Robert ignored her. "Take your clothes off," he commanded, flinging his white lab coat on the floor.

She glared at him, her hands balled into fists at his nerve. "You've got to be kidding!"

He looked at her over his shoulder as he adjusted the water in the large shower cubicle. "Get a move on, woman, we don't have much time." He had the audacity to wink at her while he was unbuttoning his shirt. "This stuff is hardening up fast."

"A gentleman would leave the room!"

"What gives you the idea I'm a gentleman?" He closed the amber-tinted glass door and admonished her again. "Now if you don't start removing those clothes I'm going to have the intense pleasure of trying to pry them off you."

"You *did* do this on purpose!"

His eyes twinkled at her and the silly grin on his goo-covered face only enraged her more. "I freely admit I've wanted to see you naked since the first time we met," he said, removing his shirt, "but the idea of covering you in glop to achieve that goal never even occurred to me." He shook his head slowly. "I guess I'm not as inventive as I thought."

He bent over to take off his shoes and gave Maggie a clear view of his broad, powerful torso. The muscles along his back flexed with each movement, strong and well defined, enticing her to step over and touch them. She fought the insane urge, frozen in her tracks by the sudden realization that he was quite serious about forcing her into the shower with him.

"Maggie, love," he crooned teasingly, "if you don't start undressing I'm going to have a great time trying to peel your panties off."

"Mind your own business," she ordered curtly, attempting to cross her arms over her chest. The cream was getting less pliable by the minute, making her clothes feel like a straitjacket.

"You are part of my business, remember?" he taunted, unzipping his jeans and stepping clumsily out of the wet, stiff legs. "Alison would never forgive me if I turned her best temp into a statue." His navy-blue briefs were the only thing left now, his unclad form hard, tanned, and impossibly tantalizing. "Need some help?" he inquired politely.

"No!" His body alone was distracting enough. If he started to put his talented fingers where they didn't belong again all her good intentions would go straight down the drain. "You just stay away from me."

"I could—"

"Get in the shower," she ordered.

He slipped his thumbs into the waistband of his briefs. "Can't wait to see the rest, Maggie?"

"Stop right there!" She spun away from him and slowly counted to ten. "Are you in yet?"

"No." He was so close she could feel his warm breath on the back of her neck. "Mmm, you smell good. I may have made a mistake in the formula somewhere, but at least I got the fragrance right."

"Robert! I'm not getting into that shower with you and that's that. I'm not kidding."

"I'm not kidding either, Maggie," he whispered in her ear, grabbing hold of the bottom of her yellow sweatshirt. "This stuff may harden completely any moment." With one quick, efficient movement he stripped the top off her and dropped it on the floor.

"All right!" she gasped in exasperation. "But I can undress myself, thank you very much." It took both hands to clutch her bra in place. "Now get in there and close the door. And no peeking." The heat of his body seemed to be calling out to her, tempting her unmercifully.

"Me? Peek?" he replied with exaggerated innocence. "A gentleman wouldn't do such a thing. And don't forget about your hair, we wouldn't want it to fall out." Chuckling evilly, he ran a slippery finger down her warm spine.

She whirled around to face him. "You're kidding?"

"I hope so." He shrugged his shoulders, then strolled toward the running water, completely unconcerned with his nakedness. "How about you? Are you peeking?"

She was, and his taunt made her blush from head to toe, but at the moment she had more important worries on her mind. "Robert, answer me! My hair . . ."

He was already closing the cubicle door. She could hear him humming with pleasure as he stepped under the tingling spray of warm water and started to rinse himself. Maggie thought about how it would feel to wash off the gook covering her and knew there weren't any options left. She was going to have to get in there with him; he certainly wasn't going to hurry so she could take a separate shower.

It would work out just fine if he kept his hands off her—and if she could resist the temptation to touch him. With great haste she awkwardly stripped off the rest of her gummy, stiff clothes and opened the shower door. Keeping her eyes averted from his tanned body would be quite a challenge.

"Keep your back turned," she demanded, quite pleased with herself for managing to keep her voice even. There had been an accident in the lab, and they were simply following emergency procedures.

"Yes, ma'am."

"And your hands to yourself."

Splashing water was the only sound in the tiled shower. "Agreed?" Maggie asked again.

In lieu of an answer he held up a bottle behind his back. "Shampoo?" he offered, standing to one side of the large stall. "Better wash your hair," he added sternly as he began lathering his own.

The water hit her with full force and she drenched her hair completely, the feeling so marvelous she knew wild horses couldn't drag her away now. She squeezed a dollop of liquid out on her hand and began shampooing her tangled locks, careful not to touch or even look at him. It took two washings and a thorough final rinse, but at last her hair felt clean again. She sighed with relief.

"There. All done."

"Good," he said, turning to face her. "By the

way, I was kidding about your hair falling out. I just wanted to get that part out of the way so we wouldn't have soap in our eyes when we started fooling around."

"You—you—"

Robert grinned. "You're beautiful when you splutter. Here," he added, handing her a bar of soap, "it'll be much easier to get all this cream off if we help each other."

He was doing it again, she thought with exasperation, making it her choice. It was as if he knew she didn't have the willpower to resist him. Water was cascading over them, enclosing them in a warm cocoon. Feeling desire spring to life within her, Maggie rubbed the bar of soap between her hands, keeping her eyes fixed on his chest.

One finger lifted her chin as his mouth came down to close gently over hers. Her body betrayed her need, the first kiss leading to a much deeper one before he raised his head to look into her eyes. Only their lips had touched, but they both knew they wanted so much more than just that simple caress. The knowledge arced between them like a current of electricity. They knew the point of no return was fast approaching.

Robert reached out, taking her hands and placing them on his chest. That was all it took. She slid her fingers up over his shoulders and down his arms, tracing the flow of bubbles across his glistening torso. Touching, cleansing, getting to know the feel and texture of his skin, Maggie played a sensual game beneath the steady stream of warm water, steam surrounding them in a gentle cloak.

Leaning back against the wall, he let her explore to her heart's content, watching the gentle sway of her breasts as she skimmed her hands down his legs, curved around his calves, and started with his feet. Each leg was thoroughly soaped before she advanced back up him.

"Let me," he whispered hoarsely, reaching for the soap. If he had to endure much more of her intimate touch he knew his self-control would be lost. His entire being ached with desire for her.

Maggie watched as he rubbed the bar slowly between his hands, anticipation coursing through her body at the look of hungry warmth in his gray eyes. She felt herself quiver before he even touched her, her nipples hardening beneath his gaze.

"Turn around," he commanded softly.

Complying with his wish, she gasped aloud as his touch began to rekindle the fires that had been smoldering inside of her since last night. He slid his hands along the curve of her back, down over her smooth, well-shaped derriere, sculpting her full hips as if memorizing every enticing curve. Starting with her feet, he worked his way up past one slender knee to curve around a water-slick thigh, then slid back down to begin anew on her other leg.

Maggie collapsed against him as he slid his hands up the front of her body, teasing her softly rounded belly before lightly brushing across her femininity. "Robert . . ."

"I'm not done yet," he teased, slipping his hands between them to cup her breasts. "We wouldn't want them to not have the same care as everything else." He proceeded to lavish them with attention.

She moaned as he teased each one in turn, the lightly callous pads of his thumbs moving back and forth across the exquisitely sensitive tips.

Finally he turned off the flow of water spewing over them. "I pronounce us squeaky clean," he said, pressing their hips intimately into each other. "Have you had enough?"

"Yes . . . no!" Her voice trembled with emotion.

"My sentiments exactly." He helped her out of the cubicle and enclosed their bodies in a huge fluffy brown towel. "Come to bed with me?"

"Yes," she whispered, trembling as much from the awareness of what was to come as the cool air on her skin. Clinging to him for support, her face buried in his neck, she wanted him with a longing she'd never felt before. Her eyes widened when he led her to a cozy bedroom. "But I . . ."

"Shh, I'll take care of everything. Come with me," he coaxed, drawing her with him as he eased down on the bed. His lips covered hers, his tongue plunging deeply as he gathered her close. Again and again he tasted of her, possessed her, claimed the sweet cavern of her mouth as his and his alone. His hand drifted down to caress her intimately, his gentle, knowing touch arousing her to inflaming heights.

"Oh, please," she moaned, moving sensuously against him, wanting to feel all of him.

Then his body covered hers, and she could feel him, hard and strong and demanding. Gone was his teasing, his game of letting her lead, replaced by a masculine desire Maggie met with eager willingness. They came together slowly, savoring the moment, holding in check a raging passion that threatened to overwhelm them in its demand for fulfillment.

The spiraling peak went round and round, faster and faster, until it shattered suddenly and she started to fall. She was floating on air, flying down through the clouds, the warmth of the sun around and inside her. She felt him collapse beside her, his ragged breath music to her ears as he wrapped her tightly in his arms.

"You're beautiful," he whispered, planting small kisses down the slender column of her throat.

"Stop," she objected halfheartedly, feeling his hard eagerness returning. She tried to wiggle away.

Tremors shook his body, bursting forth into hearty laughter as she continued to struggle. "You've got to be kidding," he said, still chuckling to himself. "You're rubbing every inch of your body against mine."

Suddenly quiet, she grinned mischievously and met his desirous gaze. "How's this?" she asked, refusing to move a muscle no matter how he coaxed and stroked her.

Robert patted her shapely buttocks and chuckled, rolling her over to begin anew. "I never could resist a challenge, Maggie, especially a lovely challenge like you."

CHAPTER EIGHT

"I only came down here to find out what you wanted for lunch," Maggie said, snuggling in Robert's arms, blissfully content.

Robert hugged her close. "See what a great bargain you got? You also found ecstasy beyond your wildest dreams."

"Pretty confident, aren't you?"

"Original too," he teased. "Who else would give you a total body massage with a just-invented cream before they got down to . . . uh, business."

"Business!" She poked him in the chest. "You call this business?" Her hazel eyes sparkled with enjoyment.

"My favorite kind." He kissed her softly. "Admit it, we were incredible together," he murmured, nibbling on her lips. "You're delicious. Just what I wanted for lunch."

"Speaking of which . . ." Maggie trailed off, laughing as their empty stomachs spoke to each other.

Robert patted her belly affectionately. "Don't

worry, we'll feed you soon." He slipped out of bed and opened the closet door. "First things first."

Though momentarily distracted by the sleek lines of his body, reality struck her. "My clothes! What am I going to wear?" she asked, sitting up and wrapping the sheet around her.

"That looks pretty good to me." He leered at her. "I have you trapped and at my mercy."

"Robert, be serious."

A royal blue cotton robe landed on the bed. "Wear that for now," he said, stepping into a clean pair of jeans.

"And later?" she inquired, slipping on the robe. It swamped her, the hem brushing along her ankles and the cuffs covering her hands. She made the necessary adjustments and belted the robe around her waist.

"I'll throw our clothes in the washer while we eat and see what happens."

"You have a washing machine here?"

He smiled at her. "And a dryer."

"Why?" A puzzled expression crossed her face.

"Having experienced one of my experiments firsthand, need you ask?"

"I see your point. It's just that I'm surprised you wash your own clothes. Isn't that part of your housekeeper's duties?"

"Not when it comes to disasters like those in the bathroom. The last time I took clothes like that home they destroyed the machine and Inez threatened to leave me," he explained, shaking his head with remorse. "She'll never let me live that one down."

"You could always get a new housekeeper."

"Are you kidding? You've seen what I can do to an office in a matter of a few weeks. Housekeepers who can put up with me don't grow on trees, you know." He shrugged his shoulders. "Besides, I like her. She's temperamental—quite a character, actually—but then so am I, I suppose."

"You suppose?" Maggie teased.

Robert glared at her. "I tolerate her eccentricities because she's a superb cook," he added in his own defense. "And she puts up with mine because I'm so charming."

"Ha! I've seen your files, remember? She tolerates you because you pay her well and let her have so much time off."

"Everybody isn't as mercenary as you are, dear."

"Mercenary?" Maggie objected in outrage.

"I suppose you're going to stand there and tell me you're not going to use this little accident as a means to clinch your hazardous duty pay?"

"Well . . ."

Robert laughed triumphantly. "See? Mercenary."

"That's not being mercenary. That's simply looking out for my own best interests." Maggie glanced at the clothes lying in a heap on the bathroom floor. "I'll have you know that was a designer sweatshirt. And those are French running

shoes," she said haughtily. "I'll give you an item-
ized bill Monday morning."

"Now don't you start in on me," he said, then
quickly changed the subject. "How about a
pizza?"

"With everything?"

"No little fishes are allowed on my pizza."

She pretended to pout but couldn't abide ancho-
vies either. "Very well. In the spirit of interoffice
harmony, I capitulate. But no bell peppers either."

"Anything else, madam?"

"Just order the thing, will you? Or I'll have you
for lunch instead."

"Mmm. I think I like your idea better."

"Make the call," she commanded, closing the
bathroom door in his face.

Combing her tangled hair out was no easy task,
but she felt much better when that was accomplished. Then a loud knock sounded on the door.
She grinned at his formality.

"Yes?"

"May I come in?"

"Enter." Robert walked into the room with a
pair of large tongs in his right hand. She was almost afraid to ask, but curiosity won. "What are
those for?"

He chuckled. "Don't tempt me."

Opening the bifold doors on the opposite side of
the shower, he revealed a stacked washer and
dryer. He started the machine and then used the

tongs to pick up each piece of clothing, dropping them carefully in the swirling, soapy water.

"Clever, very clever."

He took a deep bow. "Thank you. It took many hours of research to come up with that solution." A loud gong echoed through the warehouse. "Saved by the bell."

"What is that horrible noise?"

"Our doorbell. I told you we'd know well in advance if anybody showed up."

Maggie wrapped the oversized robe more securely around her despite his assurances. "Who's here?"

"Salvation, stimulation, and sustenance."

"Sounds like a law firm."

"No, a pizza."

They sat companionably at a counter in the studio apartment's kitchen and ate every last morsel, including a mixed green salad Robert had thoughtfully ordered. Maggie had never seen him so happy, and never felt so happy herself. But she was well aware their good mood had little to do with full stomachs.

Maggie knew she should be worried about the intimate turn their relationship had taken, but somehow managed to push her doubts aside. It seemed like destiny that they should be lovers. From the moment they met a fire had smoldered between them, culminating in the pleasure they had just shared. She realized that come what may, they were destined to share such ecstasy again and again. She couldn't fight the emotions growing between them any longer even if she wanted to. Robert was right, they were good together.

"We should have ordered two," he said as he finished off the last slice.

"I'd never get into my jeans if you had."

"But that robe is roomy enough for two."

She backed away from him and held the empty carton between them, recognizing the sudden sparkle in his eyes. "Shouldn't the clothes be about ready for the dryer?"

"Not yet," he replied, taking the box from her and dropping it on the counter. Grinning, he advanced on her as she backed out of the kitchen.

"Now, Robert. We have business to take care of."

"Yes, we do, now that we've revived and refueled—"

"Real business," she interrupted hastily.

"This is real," he murmured, encircling her waist with his arms and pulling her close. "Very real, sweet Maggie. Let me show you."

A loud, irritating buzzer blared throughout the room. His arms went slack and a scowl appeared on his face when the sound didn't stop. "Time to put the clothes in the dryer," he cursed, leaving the room and mumbling about lunatics who designed timers that didn't cut off by themselves.

Maggie quickly cleared the remains of their repast, then dashed upstairs to get some puzzling papers she had found earlier. Destiny may have taken a hand here this afternoon, but that didn't mean she was prepared to allow her desires—or his—to control her completely.

She wasn't fooling herself for an instant. Balancing business and pleasure wouldn't be easy. If this situation was going to work, Robert had to realize that she was still his secretary. He was a one-in-a-million man, this was a one-in-a-million job, and if at all possible she intended to hold onto both.

Coming back into the apartment, she held up a thick stack of papers for his inspection, doing her best to appear businesslike while wearing his ill-fitting robe.

"Back to work," she said firmly.

"What are those?"

"You tell me." She rattled off a few incomprehensible titles.

Robert sighed. "Bring them over here."

He was seated at the counter, looking so masculine and self-confident Maggie was hesitant to go near him. She chose to stand on the opposite side of the counter, out of his reach and the almost tangible aura of male power surrounding him. Why was she having so much trouble getting her mind back on work?

Because things were happening too fast, she realized. She needed time to assimilate all the changes their lovemaking had brought about in their relationship, time to get used to the idea of being two people at once. That was what was required: one Maggie at work, another away from work. Robert would understand that. Wouldn't he?

"Great! This is some of the Trescott file," he announced, holding out some papers to her.

Maggie sighed. He did understand. She stepped closer and examined the papers. "How do you know?" she asked, flipping through to the last page. "There isn't one mention of Trescott on any of these."

"That's the name of the company. It's the description of the product that tells me what they go to," he explained patiently.

No one could possibly think like he did. "A normal person would put the name of the company down at least once," she said shaking her head in amazement at his thought process.

He was a brilliant man, but sometimes she wondered if the marbles were all there. Still, despite his chaotic methods, he seemed perfectly capable of attaining his goals. Proof in point: His goal had been her and he had most certainly gotten her. Such determination was a little bit frightening.

Though he fixed her with a sidelong glance, Robert chose not to respond to her jibe. Gathering up another set of papers, he identified them as part of another file and put them aside. Maggie was impressed by the way he quickly sorted through the stack. But when he came to the last three sheets a puzzled frown appeared on his face.

"Where did you find these?" he asked, scrutinizing them uneasily.

"I don't know for sure."

He gave her a piercing look, pinning her in place with his eyes. "Try to remember, it's important."

She thought back to this morning and what she'd done. "I think they were part of that stack on the floor by the last filing cabinet, over in the corner." She tried not to wince under the flash of hardness in his steady gaze. "Well, I'm sorry, but I'm not absolutely positive," she added defiantly. "What's the big deal?"

"They're part of the Trescott file, too, but . . . never mind. I'll keep these down here," he replied, suddenly distant. He walked toward the bathroom. "Your clothes are probably dry by now."

Maggie barely squeezed into her jeans. "Lord, trust a man to put everything in a hot dryer. I hope they stretch," she muttered, slipping on her lemon-yellow sweatshirt and pulling it down low over her hips. "Not too bad." Luckily she hadn't let him near her shoes, so even though they were dirty they still fit.

The so-called living room was empty when she came out of the bathroom, so she returned to the office and found Robert half under a desk going through some more papers on the floor. "Need any help?"

"Have you touched any of these piles over here?"

"No, I thought I'd finish the boundaries first," she said, pouring herself a cup of coffee.

He looked up at her for the first time and his eyes opened wide at the sight. "I like the fit of those jeans."

She grinned, glad to see he'd gotten over whatever had been bothering him a moment ago. "What about your lab?" she reminded him, tugging at her top and sitting down behind a desk. "Shouldn't we call in a clean-up crew?"

"Oops. I was having so much fun I forgot about that," he said, standing up hurriedly. "I'd better call them before that stuff gets so hard it won't scrape off." He looked as if he was afraid to pick up the phone. "Ted is going to love this."

An hour later, Ted Myers was surveying the damage, laughing heartily. He looked absolutely beside himself with joy at the prospect of earning Saturday double time for cleaning up the accident in Robert's lab.

"Well, Ted," Robert asked in a worried tone, "what do you think?"

"I think I'm going to start selling tickets to these messes of yours," the small but strongly built maintenance man replied. He shook his head in disbelief as he looked around the workshop. "I'd make a mint."

Maggie was laughing too. "Just be thankful you didn't have a front row seat."

"It wasn't that bad!" Robert objected.

"Of course not. Everybody spends their Saturdays impersonating a bowl of cottage cheese," she shot back.

Ted was holding his sides, laughing fit to burst. "I love it! She's just what you need, Robert. Someone to keep you in line when I'm not here. Of course, from the looks of this place I may as well take up residence."

"I take it you've dealt with his catastrophes before, Ted?" she asked.

He nodded. "You should have seen the last one. There was this slippery green slime all over the—"

"I'll have you know," Robert interrupted with a superior air, "that product eventually turned into a real money-maker."

"As what?" Ted wanted to know. "The lead character in a horror movie?"

Maggie snapped her fingers in recognition. "The Slippery project." She winked mischievously at Ted. "He sold it to a company that ships machine parts overseas. Evidently, it's a rust preventative superior to the one they were using."

"No wonder I haven't had any trouble with rust on my tools lately," Ted noted thoughtfully. "But I'm not complaining. The way he's been going lately, I'll be able to retire soon."

"Enough!" Robert fixed them both with a withering stare. "I knew I should never have introduced you two." He pointed at Ted. "Get to work, you robber."

"Yes, boss," he said good-naturedly, leaving the room to get his crew and laughing all the way.

"And you," Robert added, turning to Maggie, "can insult me on your own time. Say, over a late dinner?"

She grinned. "Sorry. I've got a previous appointment."

"With whom?" he demanded.

"Alison," she replied, immensely pleased with his jealous tone of voice. "We're going to a baby shower."

"Skip it."

"I'm helping Alison play hostess. They just might notice I'm not there," she said dryly.

Robert sighed. "Go ahead, abandon me."

"How about a picnic tomorrow?"

"Excellent idea," he replied, his expression brightening immediately. "A romantic repast in the country. What time shall I pick you up?"

"Noon." She smiled, then picked up her purse and started out the door.

He caught her and trapped her against the wall. "Don't I get a good night kiss?" he murmured.

"Regardless of what happened earlier, Robert," she told him seriously, "this is still a place of business."

"Nobody's looking," he coaxed.

She sighed. "One."

"Two." He covered her mouth with his. "Are you sure I can't come home with you?" he asked when he finally let her up for air.

"Baby shower, remember?"

Robert grumbled, but he released her. "Don't catch anything."

"Babies aren't a virus, dear. You know perfectly well how you get them."

He chuckled throatily. "Stay home tonight and refresh my memory."

"Robert!"

"All right. I'll see you tomorrow," he whispered, kissing her again.

"Tomorrow."

James Trescott stood looking out his office window at the glittering Saturday night traffic on the street far below. Date night in the big city. Thousands upon thousands of people used his company's products every day, but weekend evenings were especially lucrative for a personal products firm. Women used a bit more makeup, men splashed on an extra dose of cologne, both sexes used hair spray, deodorant, and one kind of lotion or another to make their skins touchably soft. Courting was big business.

Without turning around, Trescott addressed a tall, thin man who was helping himself to a drink from the well-stocked bar in the corner of the plush office suite.

"You're sure about this?"

"Dead sure, Mr. Trescott. One of my operatives has been tending the plants at Chapman Corporation for the past—"

"I don't care about your methods," Trescott interrupted. "The necessity of using services such as yours may be a fact of life in this business, but I don't want the details."

The thin man shrugged. "Whatever you say, Mr. Trescott. At any rate, the information is valid. Of course, since the labs are off limits to all but the most trusted Chapman personnel, it will take some, shall we say, extraordinary measures to find out if the face-lift cream formula is identical."

"It's vital I know," Trescott said curtly.

"I understand that, sir." He grinned, knowing that at this very moment an operative of his was in the process of employing the extraordinary measures he'd mentioned to gather the information Trescott needed. "We're working on it."

"Good."

Trescott sighed and ran his slender fingers through his full head of silver-gray hair. He was a handsome man, of medium build, with blue eyes that spoke of his sharp business mind. Proud of his company and full of belief in the products he sold, he often wished this kind of espionage wasn't so prevalent these days. But it was, and if his firm was to survive he had to use every tool his competition did, whether he found it personally distasteful or not.

"I suppose it's possible they've simply beaten you to the punch, sir," the thin man continued. "Happens quite often in this business as well as others. The theory of concurrent creativity, I believe the eggheads call it."

Trescott turned from the window, his jaw set, his eyes full of determination. "I don't hold with that theory, nor do I believe in coincidences. The Chapman Corporation is fighting its way back from the mismanagement of that idiot, Dennis Chapman, and they're hungry," he said, a touch of steel in his voice. "I'm trying very hard to believe they're not hungry enough to infringe on a pending patent, but I'm not going to bet on it, not with the amount of money this face-lift cream can generate. And the fact remains that the inventor, Robert Langley, has legal ownership of the idea and has contracted those rights to us."

"That and a quarter will buy you a cup of coffee if Chapman manages to get the product out before you can bring charges."

"Exactly. The public doesn't follow court cases, they follow advertising. If Chapman's first out with the cream, our legal rights won't amount to a hill of beans. Trescott Labs will appear the copycat and therefore suspect as far as the consumers are concerned." He glared at the other man. "I need proof they've somehow managed to steal this idea. And that is what I hire you for."

His thin face calm, the industrial spy simply nodded thoughtfully. "If it's there, you'll get it. We're checking into this mysterious guy who's been dealing so secretively with Dennis Chapman." He grinned. "Should know everything there is to know about him by the middle of next week."

"Why so long?"

"Things like this take time, Mr. Trescott. Not everybody works weekends like you and I."

Trescott cleared his throat irritably. "I know. I have to wait until Monday morning to contact Robert Langley myself. There's no answer at his lab and his damn fool housekeeper won't even pass on a message to him. Says he's been working too hard."

"Has it occurred to you he may be avoiding you on purpose? I mean, if the cat has been let out of the bag somewhere, why not at the source?"

"That's just plain crazy. Langley is the most respected, reputable man in the business. He came to us with the idea, got funding to continue experimentation on his own. And his ideas are like children to him; he won't let go of them until they're prepared to meet the world head-on," Trescott replied impatiently. "He might hold a product back until he's satisfied and we're ready to kill him, but he wouldn't double-deal us."

"Still . . ."

"Forget it."

"Whatever you say, sir."

The thin man finished his drink, set the empty glass on the bar, and turned to leave. A troubled frown marring his handsome features, James Trescott watched him cross the room until he reached the door.

"Wait."

"Sir?"

The words left a bad taste in his mouth, but Trescott ordered, "All right. Keep tabs on Langley too."

CHAPTER NINE

As she drove to the home of Alison's parents, Maggie was so lost in thought she was scarcely aware of her surroundings. Things were moving along too quickly between her and Robert. When she was near him she couldn't think straight; when she was away from him she became even more confused about their future together—if indeed they even had one.

This baby shower was just what she needed to take her mind off her muddled thoughts. Alison would be the only problem she would have to deal with tonight. Knowing her as well as she did, however, Maggie was prepared for her friend's relentless quest for all the juicy details.

Struggling out of the car with her present and boxes of party decorations, Maggie weaved up to the front door, nearly tripping on the steps. Her precariously balanced packages threatened to fall when the door opened unexpectedly.

"Help!"

"Maggie, are you in there?"

"Cute, Alison." She shifted the load again. "Don't just stand there giggling. Help me!"

Alison reached for one of the boxes. "I'll take—"

"Not that one!" Maggie made a diving catch for her gift as the rest of the packages tumbled from her arms. "Honestly, Ali! I'll bet you're the type who takes the bottom cantaloupe from a produce display."

"You could have made more than one trip," Alison teased, crawling around on the floor to retrieve the rolls of colorful crepe paper.

Maggie set her present down carefully before surveying the cluttered floor. "Oh, Lord, it's catching." Paper cups, plates, and decorations were scattered across the entry hall.

"What is?"

"Messiness!" she cried in dismay.

Alison sat back on her heels and looked up at her friend slyly. "Really? And how *is* Robert?"

"Robert who?"

"You don't fool me for a minute. The only person we both know who makes messes is your new boss," she retorted, standing up with her arms full. "Have you been involved in any, um, interesting experiments yet?"

Maggie saw the mischief in her friend's eyes and quickly changed the subject. "Are we going to have the party in the family room?" she asked, picking up the last of the fallen items and looking for a place to put them.

Alison led the way, talking all the while. "I'm going to get every little tidbit out of you before the night is through, Maggie," she promised with a grin. "But for the moment I'll grant you a reprieve. We have to get this room decorated." She dumped her load on the couch and rubbed her hands together. "Later," she whispered mysteriously, "you'll tell all."

Maggie ignored her. "What do you want to start with?"

"Crepe paper. Let's twist these strands together and string them from the ceiling fan to all the walls. Did you remember to bring some tape?" she asked, unwrapping the rolls of baby-blue, soft pink, and pale yellow paper.

Maggie dug through the pile on the couch and pulled out the tape. "Did you doubt me?" she asked, threatening Alison with the package.

"You? The master of organization? Never!" She got down on her knees, her hands folded together and raised. "Forgive me," she pleaded dramatically.

Maggie laughed. "Cut it out, Ali, we have work to do," she ordered, tossing the tape at her. "I'll string, you stick."

"Your wish is my command."

They worked companionably, twisting and stringing the paper and decorating the rest of the room. When they were done Maggie collapsed on the couch and surveyed the results. The colors

155

flowed out from the center of the room, creating a carousel effect.

"You don't think it's too much, do you?" Alison asked from her position on the floor.

"No, I think it's great. And no one deserves this more than Marilyn."

"She's a strong woman," Alison murmured somberly.

"Very." Maggie thought of all their friend had been through and how uncomplicated her own life had been until recently. "I don't know if I could be as tough."

"Me either." She sat up and looked at Maggie. "We haven't even been married once and she's already lost a husband and found another. I hope this baby's all right," Alison murmured, thinking of the one Marilyn had miscarried right after the car accident.

"I talked to her two days ago," Maggie replied. "Her doctor told her she's doing fine. About time too. She's more than ready to start a family."

"Maggie, do you ever worry about getting older and not having a husband or children yet?"

"We're only twenty-six, for heaven's sake! We have plenty of time."

Alison sighed. "I suppose. But we're not getting any younger. Our parents already had us by the time they were twenty-six."

"Well, they had an advantage." Maggie thought of her parents, happily married for so many years. She'd have to go see them again soon. Tucson was only a short plane ride away. "They found each other earlier in life."

"Don't you want to have kids?"

"Yes. But not alone. I want someone to grow with, who'll stick with me through everything life throws our way." She shrugged her shoulders. "I want it all, just like our parents."

"So do I," Alison murmured. "And I'd like it soon."

So would she, Maggie thought, her mind turning to Robert and the feelings growing between them. She sighed, then noticed Alison gazing at her curiously. "Come on, lazybones," she said, jumping up and walking over to the door. "There's still work to be done to get this party in gear."

"What's in the box?" Ali asked, peering at Maggie's present for Marilyn.

Maggie laughed at her insatiable curiosity. "Guess."

"Give me a hint," she demanded, picking up the large box and shaking it.

"Don't rattle it!" Maggie ordered, taking the present away from her. "It might break."

Alison glared at her. "That's not much of a hint."

Maggie carried the present into the family room. "It's bigger than a bread box," she teased, setting it down gently on a table.

"Hmm," her friend murmured thoughtfully as her delicate fingers skimmed over the wrapping paper.

"You wouldn't dare!"

Alison grinned mischievously as she fingered the taped edges. "Do you want to bet?"

"Okay, I'll tell you," she said in exasperation, slapping Alison's hands away from the package. "Knowing you, you'd manage to open it and look inside without leaving a trace."

"Years of practice."

"It's a replica of that sculpture we saw at the mall, the one Marilyn liked so much."

"A mother with her newborn infant, suckling at her breast?" Alison asked. Maggie nodded. "How sweet! She really wanted that sculpture."

"I couldn't afford the original, but I think she'll be pleased by this," Maggie agreed. "Now that your curiosity has been assuaged, let's get back to work." The doorbell rang. "Oh, no!" Maggie exclaimed. She pointed a finger at her. "Now, see what you've done? All your dillydallying and we're not even ready."

"Forgive me! I've ruined your reputation! Whatever will our guests think?"

"They'll think you're a loon, that's what."

Alison winked at her. "Or maybe they'll think your new boss has you all in a dither."

"They don't even know about him."

"Yet," Ali said, chuckling gleefully.

Maggie's eyes widened. "Alison, don't you dare!"

But her fears proved needless. The party went quite well, Alison managed to keep her mouth shut about Robert, and afterward everyone even pitched in to clean up. When all the guests had gone, the pair sat down and breathed a happy sigh of relief. There was only one thing left to do, and after she'd rested for a moment Maggie struggled out of her seat and began to take down the crepe paper.

Alison was less energetic. "I'm ready for my vacation," she mumbled. "Just think, two weeks of clear blue water, sandy white beaches, the blazing sun, and lots of handsome men." The thought seemed to bolster her strength and she got up to help with the paper. "Doesn't it sound like fun, Maggie?"

"Yes." Especially if Robert was there with her.

"You could still change your mind and come with us. We don't leave for another week."

The "us" she was referring to were four other women who also worked for the temporary agency. Maggie realized her attitude had changed so much in the last few days that the thought of hanging around on a beach with four women watching men stroll by hardly thrilled her. Now, if Robert strolled by . . .

"I'm on a job, remember?" Maggie wanted to take back the words as soon as they left her mouth.

"Ah, yes, Robert Langley. Had any good messes lately?"

She might as well get it over with, Maggie decided. Alison wouldn't let up until she'd wormed something out of her. "Funny you should ask,"

Maggie murmured, launching into an abbreviated version of her day.

Alison sat listening attentively, her eyes opening wider as the story progressed. "You're kidding?"

"No, the cream really did spew everywhere."

"You made this up," Alison accused.

"It's the truth. Why do you think I'm being paid so much? It's hazardous duty for sure."

"Well, he did say his office was in terrible shape."

"It is, believe me. Imagine an office that's been ransacked." She rolled her eyes expressively. "This one is worse."

Alison shuddered at the thought. "It's beyond my scope to even imagine working in such a place." She eyed her friend slyly. "But you obviously love it."

"It's quite a challenge," Maggie replied, refusing to rise to the bait.

"How did you get the stuff off?" she asked, then added innocently, "Did Robert help you?"

Maggie could feel the warm glow of a blush cover her face. "Well, we were covered from head to toe and—"

"Ah-ha!" Alison crowed, jumping to her feet excitedly. "I knew it. Is this serious?"

"I don't know," Maggie murmured. "It's all too new, too soon to tell anything yet."

"But you want it to be," her friend stated with knowing conviction. "Don't you?"

Maggie held up her hands helplessly. "I don't

know, Ali. We're so different, almost complete opposites."

"They say opposites attract. I'd love to find out for myself. Heck, I'd like to find someone period."

"You're in too much of a hurry, Ali," she warned. "You'll get into trouble that way."

"Trouble?" Her eyes widened innocently. "As in . . ."

Maggie shook her head. "You're hopeless."

"Tell me something I don't know."

"Oh, Ali, I didn't mean—"

"It's all right, don't worry about it." She sighed. "Tonight, when everyone was parading pictures of their children around . . . I guess it just got to me."

"Don't worry. You'll have pictures of your own someday."

"I know." She wadded up some more paper for the trash. "And stop changing the subject. What are you going to do about this wild, passionate attraction you have for Robert Langley?"

"I didn't say that!"

Alison patted her on the back. "You didn't have to. I'm your friend, remember?"

"Then stop the inquisition. I really don't know what I'm going to do. Bide my time, I guess."

"Well, when are you seeing him next?"

Maggie suddenly felt very tired and even more unsure of her future. "We're going on a picnic tomorrow."

"That's more like it," Ali said, nodding her head

sagely. "Now you go on home and get a good night's sleep. And don't worry about me. I can wait until next week for all the juicy details," she teased, practically pushing Maggie toward the front door. "Who knows, by tomorrow night things could really get cooking."

Little did her friend know just how hot things already were. The experience was entirely new to Maggie. But wasn't that supposed to be what she wanted? New experiences, new challenges? Tomorrow was a new day, and she had no idea what it would bring—save the undeniable fact that Robert would be an important part of whatever happened.

"Are you sure you know where we're going?" Maggie asked, looking out the car window at the unfamiliar scenery they were whizzing past.

"Almost there," Robert assured her as he slowed the powerful sports car to take a sharp right onto a bumpy dirt road. It took all his concentration to keep his eyes on the road and not on the lovely skin exposed by Maggie's deliciously brief white tank top and red shorts.

She quoted a sign they passed as they drove along. "TRESPASSERS WILL BE EATEN, THIS MEANS YOU! Robert, what are you doing?" she asked, twisting around in her seat to stare at him.

"Don't worry, I know the owner."

"Does he know you?" she asked skeptically.

He flashed her an engaging smile. "We even have his permission."

The road soon turned into little more than a dirt path. Cows grazed on the horizon, completing the bucolic scene surrounding them. Slowing the car to a crawl, Robert picked his way carefully along the path until they finally rolled to a stop under the spreading branches of a large shade tree. When he switched off the engine, quiet descended over them like a blanket.

"What kind of person would post a sign like that?" Maggie asked, whispering and looking around cautiously though she didn't quite know why.

"Someone very serious about privacy," he replied, getting out of the car and coming around to open her door. He grinned. "But like I said, we have permission to be here. I think you can talk out loud."

Maggie stuck her tongue out at him. "You can tell this mysterious owner that his sign works. If it had been me in the driver's seat, I would have been back up that road and out of sight in nothing flat," she informed him, still not making a move to get out of the car. She eyed the fence separating them from the grazing cattle. "Are there any bulls over there?"

He gently pulled her out of the car and into his arms. "I'll protect you."

"Mmm." She willingly burrowed against him. "My strong, brave matador."

"I don't know about the bulls, but I'm certainly

seeing red," he murmured throatily, slipping his hand inside the bottom of her skimpy red shorts.

"Robert!" She sprang away from him in surprise. "What about the owner?"

"I'd introduce you, but he's not here. It's just you and me," he whispered.

Relief flooded through her at the thought, but she still pulled away from his sensual touch. "We came out here to eat, enjoy the sunshine and clean air."

"And each other." He picked up a blanket and threw it at her. "Find a spot for our picnic," he said, then added hastily at her thunderous look, "Please?"

Maggie didn't know what was wrong with her. Nervous, jumpy, he made her feel things she'd never experienced before. He made her want him with a reckless abandon that was new to her. Yesterday was still beyond her comprehension. Sensible, level-headed Maggie, making love with a man she'd only known a short time—and at work at that. What was happening to her?

Was she falling in love with him?

She had all the signs. Each day she couldn't wait to get to work and see him. A light went on inside her at the sound of his voice, and his touch made her draw upon every ounce of control she had so as not to fall into his arms.

But her feelings toward him were quickly drifting way beyond simple desire. The emotions building within her were thrilling and yet scary at the same time, reminding her to take it slowly and carefully. With Robert it would be too easy to get in over her head before she even realized she was drowning.

"Have you decided yet?" he asked dryly, chuckling at the confused expression on her face as she wandered around the shade tree.

"Right here," she informed him, shaking the soft red and black plaid blanket out over the level grassy surface.

A gentle breeze blew the spring air around them as they settled comfortably on the blanket and started to unpack their picnic lunch. The sun filtered through the branches overhead, warm and inviting on their skin.

"What did you bring?" he asked.

"You first."

He smiled at her wickedly. "Wine," he announced, showing her the label. "A corkscrew, glasses—only the best for you, my dear," he said, thumping a wineglass with his index finger. "The most expensive plastic."

"How gallant of you."

He chuckled and continued his list. "Crackers, havarti cheese, black olives, plates, napkins, grapes of a different kind," he added, holding up the green and purple fruit. "For you to feed me later while I recline in regal comfort."

"Ha!"

"Did I leave anything out?"

"I am duly awed by your thoroughness." She

opened her sack. "We also have cheddar cheese, rolls, carrot and celery sticks, more crackers, napkins, plates—"

"You didn't trust me?" he asked, a comical wounded look on his face.

"In a word, no," she retorted, taking the glass of wine he held out to her. "Quite frankly, I'm amazed we didn't have to break open the bottle of wine by bashing it on the fender of your car."

"Are you crazy? That car is a classic, my dear." He rubbed his hands together in anticipation as he looked at all the food. "Where shall we start?"

"Anywhere you want."

"You," he growled, drawing her into his arms and nibbling on her neck. "Mmm, tasty. Just what I had in mind."

"I'm going to spill my wine," she warned, holding it over his head.

"Throw it away."

His lips left a warm trail of kisses as he worked his way down to her shapely legs. Maggie carefully let a few drops of the white wine drip on him, repeating the process when it failed to stop his sensual nibbling.

"It can't be raining!" he exclaimed, looking up at the clear blue sky. At that moment she chose to let a few more drops fall, directly on his face.

Watching him splutter, she couldn't stifle the laughter bubbling within her. "You told me to throw it away."

166

"I'll get you," he threatened, tickling her sides unmercifully.

"Stop!" she gasped.

"Say you're sorry."

"I'm not sorry!" Laughing so hard she could barely see, she jumped up and ran around the tree —straight into the arms of a stranger.

He had coal-black hair, piercing emerald-green eyes, and a hardness to him that frightened her. A short scar on the side of his face from eye to ear added to his alarming demeanor.

"Oh, God," Maggie murmured.

"Not quite," he said, letting go of her. "Still can't handle your women, Langley?"

"Better than you can," he shot back, and introduced the two. "Maggie, meet Colt," he said, slipping an arm around her waist reassuringly, well aware of the alarming effect his friend had on most people. He could cut someone in two with a glance. "He owns this place."

She nodded her head in acknowledgment and he returned the gesture. "I'm taking off soon." He looked at Robert. "How's the Trescott project?"

"Brewing along."

Maggie chuckled, and the intimidating stranger's gaze shifted to her face. "Does he mean brewing or spewing?" he asked with the barest hint of a smile.

Surprised to find a sense of humor beneath the man's hard exterior, she decided he might not be so bad after all. "You must know him pretty well."

167

He simply nodded. "Hang on to this one, Robert," he said. "Anybody who's still around after one of your explosions . . ." His voice trailed off as he disappeared through the trees.

Wide-eyed, Maggie mumbled, "Strange."

"No argument. He's a good friend, though, as well as a major shareholder in Trescott Labs." Robert shrugged, shaking off his confusion at Colt's unexpected appearance and leading Maggie back to the blanket. "Are you ready to eat?"

"Ravenous," she said, plucking a grape from the cluster and popping it into her mouth.

"Where's mine?" She obligingly fed him one. "Mmm. Good. But peel the next one."

"Peel your own grapes, Caesar."

Together they filled their plates and enjoyed their feast, feeding each other in turns beneath an azure sky. Satiated at last, Maggie leaned against the tree with Robert's head in her lap, enjoying the gentle breeze and warm sunshine. She was just starting to doze off when she felt something nibbling on her midriff. Through sleepy eyes she looked at the top of Robert's head as he kissed his way up her rib cage.

"You did this on purpose," he murmured, watching her eyes flicker open.

"What?" she asked, stretching lazily beneath him.

"Wore this top without a bra," he replied, sliding the top to her chin. "So I'd have to suffer through seeing you bounce without being able to touch you."

"What's stopping you now?"

"Nothing."

His mouth closed over one puckered tip and he caressed it with his tongue. The pads of his fingers brushed across the tip of her other breast before enclosing it within his mouth, his lips hot, moist, and demanding. Marauding hands explored her curves at a leisurely pace, his mind spinning with her every sigh and moan of pleasure.

In the midst of their mutual enjoyment the sound of a helicopter taking off close by jerked them back to reality, the leaves above their heads rustling as the craft roared past.

"I'll get you for this, Colt," Robert muttered.

"It's getting late anyway," Maggie told him, sitting up and adjusting her clothes.

"We could continue in a less outdoorsy setting."

Maggie shook her head. "I told you before we left I had wash to do and such."

"Do it at my place."

"I thought you said your housekeeper was back."

"She is, but—"

Maggie cut him off with a finger on his lips, then stood up and began clearing up the remains of their meal. The mood was lost for now, and too many undecided feelings were speeding through her mind. Robert got to his feet and helped her clean up, sighing as he did so.

169

"There will be other sunny days," she promised him.

His expression brightened. "True."

"This Trescott project," she said when they had the car loaded. "What is it exactly?"

Robert frowned as he started the car and headed for home. "Why?"

"Just curious. Your friend asked about it, and you've been searching for pieces of the file."

"It's complicated," he replied hesitantly. "A two-phase project. I have a patent pending on the first phase, and the second is . . ."

"Is what?"

He glanced at her, then turned his eyes back to the road. "I repeat, why the sudden interest?"

Maggie deliberated for a moment, then decided it would be best to just explain what was bothering her. "Tell me the truth. Am I . . . are you working as hard on it as you would be if I wasn't around?"

"Maggie," Robert said with a deep sigh of relief, "is that what this is all about? Are you afraid you're keeping me from my work?" She nodded and he put his hand on her thigh, squeezing it reassuringly. "I admit you're a distraction—a very pleasant distraction—but you're a bigger help than you are a hindrance. As a matter of fact, I've been thinking of asking you how you feel about making this permanent."

"E-excuse me?" she asked, staring at him uncertainly.

"I'm not asking for an answer right now," he continued, not noticing her shocked expression. "I know you said you enjoyed temporary work. But the truth is, I need you. You've seen what I can do to a filing system. You can organize me, but the day after you leave I'll be back hip deep in my own clutter."

"Oh." Maggie tried to calm the beating of her foolish heart. She'd thought he was going to ask a question it was too soon to answer.

"I'm smart enough to know I can be ten times as productive if you stick around. So at least promise me you'll think about it, okay?" Robert asked.

What was she going to say? Everything depended on what happened between them, and at the moment she was far from certain where this amorous relationship was leading.

"All right," she managed to say. "I'll think about it."

"Good. And as far as the Trescott project is concerned," he added, "you've already helped me immeasurably. How does your skin feel today?"

"Kind of tight, now that you mention it." Then it dawned on her. "You mean . . . I thought that white glop was an accident."

"It was. The Trescott second phase is just a theoretical formula improvement, a pipe dream of mine really. I was fooling around with the first phase, mixing it with the dimly remembered ingredients from that old high school disaster you got me thinking about the other night," he explained.

"See? You were not only my inspiration, but my guinea pig as well."

"Thanks a lot!"

"A very lovely guinea pig," he assured her.

"You really know how to sweet-talk a lady, Robert."

His expression turned thoughtful. "Maybe a touch more lanolin next time. . . ."

"Not on me you don't!"

"I'll put it on by hand."

"Oh." She leaned against him and sighed. "Well, maybe just a little."

CHAPTER TEN

"I'm impressed," Maggie said as she looked around the office on Monday morning.

Ted Myers and his crew had done a nice job. Without disturbing the remaining piles of papers yet to be filed, they had managed to dust, sweep, and clean the room into submission. Even the windows sparkled, allowing the cheery rays of the morning sun to pass through unhampered by industrial grime. On the way upstairs she had noticed that the floors had been waxed, and the whole building seemed to shine.

"I'm impressed too." But Robert wasn't looking at the room. He was looking at Maggie, lovely in her usual snug-fitting jeans and an orange-colored silk T-shirt. His eyes roamed over her appreciatively. "Very impressed."

"I was referring to Ted's efficiency."

"He should be good for the amount of lip I have to put up with from him," Robert replied. "And speaking of lips, I've yet to taste yours this morning."

Maggie eluded his grasp and fixed him with a perturbed frown. "Robert, you remember what I said Friday," she told him sternly as she slipped around a desk. "This is a place of business. We have to conduct ourselves—"

"I've always wanted to chase a secretary around her desk," he interrupted, trying to grab her by the wrist. She dashed to the other side. He followed. "This is fun! Come here, you little vixen!"

"Stop it!" Maggie demanded, her angry tone belied by the grin spreading across her face. "What if someone came in? Is this the kind of professional image you want to project?" He chuckled and made another grab for her. "Well, is it?"

"Yes!" Robert grabbed again and caught her this time, pulling her into his arms. "We'll have to make this a part of our morning routine. A quick sprint around the office to get our hearts pumping."

Maggie's heart was beating fast enough already, but her pulse increased even more as Robert lowered his head to take possession of her lips. "You're crazy."

"I'm supposed to be eccentric, remember? Part of my professional image."

She stopped struggling. "Oh, what the heck," she murmured as he kissed her. Feeling herself respond to the gentle probing of his tongue, she gave in completely and met it with her own, engaging him in a pleasurable duel.

"See?" Robert asked softly. "The business world didn't come to a screeching halt."

Maggie just sighed with pleasure and kissed him again. Her mind drifted to the question he had asked her yesterday on the way back from their picnic. What would it be like to work for Robert permanently? Would every day be this crazy mixture of sensuality and hard yet satisfying work?

She knew she liked the job, was equally certain now that she was falling in love with Robert. In her way of thinking the two didn't go together, but he was doing his best to change her mind. And he almost had her convinced they could make it work. What if she said yes to his request to work for him from now on? Would his next question be more intimate, a proposal for a permanent relationship of another kind?

"That's a very unusual smile you're wearing," Robert said, stroking her cheek with his finger. "What are you thinking about?"

"Oh. I—"

The phone rang and she pulled away from him to answer it, glad for the interruption. She wasn't about to tell him the direction her thoughts were leading her, especially since she didn't know how she felt about the romantic turn they had taken herself.

"Robert Langley's office. James Trescott?" Maggie glanced at Robert. "Just a moment, Mr. Trescott, I'll see if he can be disturbed." She punched the hold button and held up the receiver.

"I love it when you talk like that," Robert said, stepping over to the desk and trying to nibble on her neck.

"Stop that!" She handed him the phone. "Here. Your public is clamoring for you."

Robert made a grab for her but she slapped his hand away, so he shrugged and sat down behind the desk to take the call. "Hello, James. I hope this isn't about the second-phase body cream." He grinned rakishly at Maggie. "I've done some initial experimentation, but I told you it might not even be possible."

"No, Robert." James Trescott's tone was worried, his voice crisp over the phone. "We have a problem."

"Your lab people aren't trying to cut corners on phase one, are they? I tried it and it won't work. Thin the stuff down too much and it—"

"It's not that either," Trescott interrupted. "It's not something I want to talk about over the phone."

"I see."

From her position by the file cabinets, Maggie could see Robert's hand tighten on the receiver, watched as his expression turned from happily distracted to very worried. The Trescott project. She wondered why everyone seemed so interested in it all of a sudden.

Robert listened intently for a few moments more, then looked sharply at Maggie. "That's not as easy as it sounds, James. I've been reorganizing the office. All right. I'll be there as soon as I can."

"What's wrong?" Maggie asked when he had hung up.

A frown furrowing his brow, Robert stood up and walked over to her. "I have to go out for a while, Maggie. When I get back I want to see every bit of information in the files even vaguely connected to Trescott Labs."

"The logs and papers in the dungeon too?" she asked, trying to erase his worried frown with a touch of humor.

He stared at her oddly for a moment before saying quickly, "No. I'll tend to those myself later. Just search this. . . ." He trailed off, looking angrily at the remaining piles of unfiled papers. "Just stay up here and find what you can. I'll be back soon," Robert finished curtly. Then he grabbed his suit coat and strode out the door.

Robert wouldn't go so far as to call James Trescott a good friend, but they had had an amiable working relationship for a number of years. They had celebrated their successful joint ventures over drinks, eaten lunch and dinner together on a few occasions, and generally enjoyed each other's intelligence. The two were alike in some ways, successful, driven men who faced life squarely and on their own terms.

But they were different too. Where Robert was easygoing, James was intense. Robert seldom worried; James had nagging stomach problems to prove he worried more than he should. At the moment, however, facing each other across the wide, cluttered desk in Trescott's office, they were both worrying as equals.

"I don't understand," Robert said as he looked at the papers in front of him again. "There are a few minor adjustments—cheaper ingredients mainly—but otherwise they've duplicated my formula molecule for molecule." He looked up at James's frowning face. "How?"

"Conjecture at this point. We're checking our own security as well as trying to, um, convince some of Chapman's people to come clean."

"And?"

"Nothing so far. None of our usually reliable snitches at Chapman has ever heard of the stuff. Just to get the formula I had to resort to a bit of skulduggery I'd rather not discuss, and as much as it sickens me, I'm even subjecting our key people to questioning."

"Have you tried confronting Chapman directly?"

James nodded. "I called the new CEO over there, Marsha Lane. Said a little birdie had told me they were gearing up to rob us and that she'd better think twice. Cool as you please, she informed me that their main thrust this year is in hair-styling products and that they left consumer rip-off garbage like face-lift creams to us. Then she hung up."

"Rip-off garbage!" Robert yelled in outrage. "Why that—I'll kill her! My formula works so well it'll turn most prunes back into plums in three months!"

Trescott had to chuckle. "Nice analogy. I'll have to remember that if Chapman doesn't cut our throats first."

"You think she was lying?" Robert asked, trying to remain calm.

"I don't know." James rubbed his hands over his face, looking very tired and haggard. "It's a moot point, really. Somebody over there has the formula and it's only a matter of time before they realize its potential and make their move. Chapman is a smaller firm; it doesn't take them as long to get things into production. We've got to stop them," he said, getting out of his chair suddenly and pacing in front of the window.

"We've got the pending patent."

"In this business having a pending patent is like being almost married, Robert, you know that. Either you've got the legal papers in hand or you don't." He stopped pacing and glared at the inventor. "What we do have, however, is your documentation of the creative process. Don't we?"

Robert shifted uneasily in his seat. "Well . . ."

"That's not the answer I want to hear, Robert. Along with evidence of their intent to infringe— evidence we're trying to get but don't have yet— we need something we can hold in front of their corporate nose, court-ready logs proving your ownership and our willingness to sue the living daylights out of them if they don't cease and desist."

"I told you, James, I'm reorganizing my files and some things have gotten misplaced." He saw the stricken look on Trescott's face and added hastily, "But I'll find them. It's my idea, too, you know. I came to you because I wanted the best company to produce my formula. I'm not about to let that slipshod operation take it from me."

James looked at him, his frown slowly disappearing. "I knew that would be the way you felt about it, Robert." He suddenly felt even worse about his decision to have the inventor checked out. "But we need that documentation as soon as possible."

"You'll get it," Robert assured him, wishing he felt as confident as he sounded. "I promise."

Maggie had seen Robert happy, comically forlorn, mildly irritated, and even downright angry, but until now she'd never seen him furious. She didn't like it one bit.

"What do you mean that's all there is?" he shouted, waving the pitifully thin Trescott file in front of her face. "Where's the copy of the patent application? Where are the funding statements, the supply lists, the expense vouchers?"

He had been morose when he came through the door, a demeanor which had quickly turned to rage when he saw how few of the sorely needed documents she'd been able to find. He had been pacing and raving like this for the last twenty minutes. Now Maggie was furious too.

"How should I know?" she demanded, raising her voice to equal the level of his. "You're the one who thinks the wastebasket is the perfect place to keep canceled checks!"

"What about the logs?" He strode over to where they were stacked neatly atop the filing cabinets. "Do you mean to tell me there wasn't anything stuck in any of them?"

"Sure there was!" she yelled back. "Gum wrappers, the cellophane from ten different kinds of candy bars, pieces of tape, labels from jars of chemicals, and lots of other things I assume you were using as bookmarks." She picked up a cardboard box from the floor and dropped it onto his desk. "Here. I saved them all. I even made note of where I found them in case you happened to have some sort of system—a particularly stupid assumption on my part, knowing you."

Her tirade seemed to quiet him for a moment, then he went off on another tangent. "I knew it," he groaned, sitting down at his desk and putting his face in his hands. "I knew your organizational frenzy would take its toll."

"Organizational frenzy!" She had to pause before she followed through on her urge to hit him. "I've been sifting through this garbage dump you called an office since I came to work here, and I've yet to even find the things you're talking about, let alone lose them." She stood right in front of him, wagging her finger threateningly. "How dare you accuse me of sabotaging your business!"

Robert looked up, his eyes gleaming fiercely. "That's just what you've done! That documentation was here before you came."

"How would you know? You couldn't even find the files for the projects you were working on the day I arrived." Maggie folded her arms over her chest and looked at him accusingly. "I'll bet you haven't seen this stuff for months, have you?"

Robert sprang to his feet. "I have too. I . . ." His voice trailed off, a disturbed expression on his face. When *was* the last time he'd seen the Trescott file intact? "Be that as it may," he continued, trying not to show his consternation, "files do not sprout legs and walk off by themselves."

"In this place?" Maggie muttered. "I wouldn't be the least bit surprised if that's exactly what happened."

"I need those papers, Maggie. They're here, and you're going to find them!" With that he strode toward the door.

"Don't tell me you're actually going to look through your rat's nest downstairs?" she asked sarcastically.

Robert's face reddened. "I am, and then I'm going home to see if maybe I left part of the file there."

"Ah-ha! Those papers have got to be here, huh?

You really don't know where they might have ended up, do you?"

"Oh, shut up," he grumbled on his way out the door.

The trouble was, he was positive the entire Trescott file had been in the office, well-buried perhaps, but there. Its disappearance was more than a minor inconvenience. In fact, in view of the situation with the stolen formula, Robert didn't like the implications of this mystery at all.

Maggie felt very alone in the warehouse. She had heard Robert clamoring around downstairs for a while, then saw him leave the building and race off in his car. Accustomed to the sounds of him puttering around while she worked, the silence now seemed profound and intimidating, leaving her feeling as empty as the workshop below. It didn't help matters any that she hadn't turned up any more of the Trescott papers and was still in the dark as to why they were so important.

She jumped and spilled her coffee when the phone rang, but managed to answer with her usual efficiency. "Robert Langley's office, may I help you?" she asked, eager to talk to somebody—anybody.

"Maggie?"

Well, almost anybody. "Yes, Mr. Langley?" she replied in a voice as cool as an arctic wind.

"Cut that out, Maggie. Have you found anything?"

"No, sir."

Robert sighed. "I've got more material here at home than I thought. I'm going to need your help sorting through it, Maggie."

"Oh?" As lonely as she was, the thought of seeing him again just now didn't thrill her. Their recent confrontation still had her upset, and she felt as if she needed this time away from him. "I suppose you could bring it in and—"

"I'd rather you come here."

"Is that really necessary?"

"I don't have the time to cart this stuff all over town, dear. Get a pencil and paper and write this down," he ordered before reeling off directions to his house. "Got that?"

"Yes, sir," she replied, then hung up on him.

Maggie was not looking forward to this meeting. An hour ago he was complaining about her efficiency, now he was saying he needed her. Which was it to be? If he couldn't live with her organizational skills then it was time for her to find another job. But what would happen to their budding personal relationship?

His place was easy to find with the concise and accurate directions he'd given her. The house was contemporary Spanish in style, quite large, with lots of smooth white walls, wide expanses of glass, and a red tile roof. The natural landscaping instead of a square green yard suited both the architecture and his personality. She approached the house slowly, nearly having to force herself up the brick walk to the front door. Finally she rang the bell.

"Maggie Johnson?"

"That's me."

So this was Robert's housekeeper. Maggie looked straight into warm brown eyes and a wide smile. The woman's white hair was pulled back into an intricate knot, framing her golden brown skin to perfection. Her skin tone and the color of her hair were deceiving, making it impossible to tell how old she really was. Forty? Fifty?

"I'm Inez. Please come in," she said in a pleasant, lightly accented voice. "You've come to put Robert in a better mood, I hope."

"Miracles aren't part of my job description."

"Nor mine." She grinned at Maggie and closed the door. "Come this way, please."

The house was open and airy, one room leading into another through curved arches and a very wide glassed-in hallway. A narrow lap-lane swimming pool was the center of a courtyard area, surrounded by the house for total privacy.

"He's in his den," Inez said, pointing ahead to another room with an open door.

Maggie smiled back at her. "Tossing me to the wolf?"

"Better you than me. He's already tried to bite my head off today," the older woman replied. "I bit him back. Lunch is almost ready," she added in parting.

Maggie hesitantly stepped into the room and

found Robert sitting behind a large, cluttered oak desk with his back to her.

"I'm here," she announced, unsure of whether to go farther into his domain or not.

He turned at the sound of her voice, then stood up, thrusting his hands into the pockets of his slacks. "I'm glad," he replied, looking as nervous as she felt.

"If you'll show me where to begin, I'll get to work while you eat your lunch."

"Maggie, I—I'm sorry about this morning," he said softly as he stepped closer to her. "You're only doing the job I hired you to do. Just have patience with me. It'll all work out." Withdrawing one hand from his pocket, he reached out to caress her neck, then slid it beneath her hair and pulled her against him.

Maggie hadn't expected an apology. It disarmed her, made her feel warm all over. "A-are you sure?"

"Yes, positive," he whispered, capturing her mouth with his.

Strong arms enclosed her tightly in his embrace, her mouth opening beneath his repeated onslaught of kisses. His tongue darted into the sweet cavern, exploring her with a thoroughness that left her breathless and wanting more.

A bell sounded in the distance. She leaned back in his arms and tried to control her erratic breathing. "Somebody's here."

"No, lunch is ready. That's Inez's polite way of

telling us. Actually," he said, slipping his arm around her waist and propelling her out of the room, "she doesn't want to intrude, especially if I'm still in a rotten mood."

"Can't say I blame her. Are you?"

He tried to slip his hand under her shirt. "I'm most definitely in the mood for you."

"Stop that," she ordered, batting his hand away. "I take it I've been invited to lunch, and I can't wait to taste Inez's cooking."

"I'd rather taste you," he whispered, pinching her on the derriere as they entered the kitchen.

She threw him an outraged glance and swept ahead of him into the spacious, modern room. The table was already set for two. "Can I help with anything?" she asked, looking at his housekeeper.

"Sit, everything is ready." She named each dish as she set it on the table. "Chicken enchiladas, Spanish rice, a tossed green salad, and my green chili!"

"It works every time," Robert murmured as Inez made iced tea for them and they filled their plates.

"What?"

"I'll tell you later," he whispered. "Go ahead, start, you don't know what you're missing."

Though Robert had said Inez had an unusual temperament, Maggie hadn't seen a trace of it yet. Maybe she was on her best behavior for company. At any rate, Maggie decided she would put up with almost anything to have cooking like this all the time. Not burning hot, the green chili was delicately seasoned and delicious.

Robert looked at Inez as she washed and dried the last pot before putting it away in one of the spacious cupboards. "Why aren't you eating with us?"

"I've already eaten. I'm going to see the babies this afternoon," she explained. "I'll be back tomorrow."

Robert nodded his head in agreement. "Be careful."

"Babies?" Maggie looked at them curiously.

"My granddaughters. Twins!" Inez announced proudly. "I'll bring some pictures back to show you," she promised.

"I'd like that."

Inez looked at Robert slyly as she packed up a container of green chili to take with her. "Of course, if you'd have some babies of your own I wouldn't have to go so far to hold little ones," she said, walking over to the door.

"Good-bye, Inez," Robert said dryly, obviously flustered by her remark. "You wouldn't want to be late."

"Think about it, you're not getting any younger," Inez admonished. She gazed happily at Robert and Maggie. "Such a handsome couple!" Then she turned and left, closing the door behind her.

Maggie could feel the heat of a blush on her cheeks from Inez's words. She casually glanced around the spotless kitchen and changed the subject, not looking at Robert. "You really live here?"

"Cut that out!" He stood up and swept her into his arms. "Or I'll be forced to throw you in the swimming pool, clothes and all."

"Put me down!"

"In the pool," he teased, "or in my bed?"

Her pulses leaped at the mention of his bed, a tingling sensation all over her body adding to her already confused emotions. Was this why he'd asked her here? "I would like to finish my lunch, please."

"Are you sure?" he asked, hugging her tighter.

"Positive!"

He returned her to her chair. "If you insist."

Maggie didn't want to insist. She was more than ready to let him carry her to his bed. But they were supposed to be working, she reminded herself, and she would insist they do so right after lunch. It wouldn't be easy, not with the way Robert was looking at her.

"What did you mean earlier when you said it works every time?" she asked, trying to break his sensual concentration.

He chuckled at her question. "Inez always makes me green chili when things are going wrong. I've been known to fake a rotten mood just to get it."

"Why don't you just try asking her to make it for you?" Maggie inquired. They were finished eating and she wanted to keep him talking.

He shook his head. "That's not the way the game is played," he replied as they loaded the dishwasher.

Would she ever understand this man? He was so direct in his approach to most things, and yet he played games with his housekeeper.

"Well, I guess we should be getting on with our sorting," she said firmly, drying her hands on a towel. He was grinning at her. "I said, we should—"

"I want to show you something," he interrupted, taking her hand and leading her into another part of the rambling house. "The master bedroom," he announced, sitting down on the bed and pulling her between his legs. "Alone at last."

"But the Trescott file . . ." She was still holding back, but tempted by the feel of his thighs against hers and the soft, inviting bed.

"I need you," he whispered, clenching the womanly curves of her buttocks in his hands and squeezing gently.

Maggie's firm resolutions about working flew out the window at his touch. She needed him too. Whatever was troubling him had caused him to explode in her direction, that was all, and now they were making up. Work would have to wait. Right now this was all she wanted to think about.

Robert reached for the hem of her silk shirt and she stepped back, pulling it over her head to show him she had changed her mind. He smiled, pulling her back into his arms, then unbuckling her tan leather belt and popping the snap on her blue jeans. With deliberate slowness he unzipped her pants, his fingers tracing the lacy softness beneath.

"Lord, you're gorgeous," he moaned, pulling her closer.

She didn't know how much longer her legs could hold her up. They were trembling with emotion, along with the rest of her. She reached down and tried to touch him.

"We have all afternoon," he whispered, stilling her hands. "Let's take it slow and easy, forget about the world for a while." His fingers were caressing her waist, slipping up to the edge of her bra, teasing her breasts before sliding around her back and down to her jeans.

She clutched his shoulders with both hands as his warm, gentle hands slipped inside the back of her jeans. Easing them down her hips, he revealed her black stretch panties. Errant fingers dipped under the edges of elastic as he traced the shape.

"Yes," she breathed, encouraging him.

Her fingers combed through his hair and clutched at his neck as he moved farther down her body. He encircled one leg with both hands and traced it from the top of her thigh to her ankle. Her body was quivering as he glided his hands across her brief undergarment, pausing to tease her before encircling her other thigh.

"Step," he murmured, helping her out of the crumpled jeans at her feet. She swayed toward the bed. "Not yet," he commanded softly, holding her in an upright position. His strong hands held her waist and pulled her toward him. His mouth moved slowly and sensuously across her naked stomach, his fingers slipping inside her briefs and caressing her.

She collapsed into his arms willingly. "Now," she whispered, her voice hoarse.

He leaned back and took her with him. "Patience."

Nibbling on the soft skin beneath his mouth, he tasted her again and again as he drifted upward, disposing of the interfering bra in his path. His lips teased her taut nipples before he followed the lines of her delicate collarbone, up her creamy throat to her mouth.

Maggie looked into his gray eyes, cradling his face in her hands, the delicate pink tip of her tongue darting out to flick at his lips, wetting them with her own. She plunged deeply into his mouth, a hot cavern of pleasure awaiting her, needing her, pulling her deeper still. With nimble fingers she started to strip him of his clothes. Impatient now to feel her beneath him, he stood up and quickly finished the job himself.

She opened her arms to him, inviting him to cover her body with his. He came to her, hard and demanding, and she enclosed him in her embrace. Her sigh of pure pleasure met his and his mouth covered hers in raging passion. They came together, already heated, pulsating with desire for one another, the flames within them escalating higher and higher until they roared to a blazing finish.

Entangled in each other's arms, they gasped for breath, capturing each other's moans of joy with swollen lips. Maggie laughed throatily, watching Robert's broad, muscular chest rise and fall as he tried to slow his breathing. She could hear the beat of his heart, soaring against her own, matching the pounding of her pulse.

She moved her head to rest on his chest. To know that she was the one responsible for its speeding beat gave her immense pleasure. As strong and powerful as he was, she could make him groan with just a touch, smiling wickedly at him as she did so.

"We're supposed to be working," she murmured, caressing the flat planes of his stomach.

"This is my kind of work. Want to take a swim?"

"I don't have a suit."

"You don't need one. It's very private out there."

"But . . ." Maggie wasn't sure she wanted to parade around naked in front of him. Making love with him was very different from casually walking out to his pool unclothed. Her sudden shyness must have seemed silly to him.

But he was smiling and whispered his understanding in her ear. "I'll even close the roof if you want."

She pulled her head up to look at him. "Close the roof?" Shy or not, her curiosity was aroused.

"I designed a system to use the pool year round." He slipped her hair behind one ear and kissed her exposed cheek. "It's even heated. Come on, I'll show you," he said, slipping out of bed and into a white terry-cloth robe. "One for my lady," he murmured, placing a similar robe beside her on the bed and turning his back.

"Thank you," Maggie replied, smiling at his sweet thoughtfulness as she slipped on the short robe. Then she took his hand and they walked out to the pool.

"The wooden shelf you see jutting out over the opposite edges of the house has two purposes," he informed her, pointing out the line. "In the winter the glass underneath comes out to enclose the entire courtyard, turning it into a greenhouse. Come summer, though, you'd bake out there under all that glass, so the windows slip back underneath and the ledges stop the sun from hitting the house directly, keeping the courtyard cool," he explained. From the look on his face, Maggie didn't have to ask to know the design was his. "The pool itself is heated by solar collectors, though in this part of the country they're scarcely needed during the spring and summer." He smiled engagingly at her. "End of lecture. Shall we swim?"

She watched as he dropped his robe and did a perfect dive into the clear blue water. Now she knew how he kept his body in shape and how he got his tan. She watched as he swam the length of the pool and back, then pushed off for another lap.

She tested the water with her big toe and found it nice and warm. Her robe joined his and she dived into the azure pool, the water soft and marvelous on her skin. She realized she couldn't remember when she'd last taken time off from work to go swimming. She was certain she'd never swam in the nude. It was deliciously erotic yet relaxing.

"I knew I could lure you in," he teased, treading water beside her and pushing his wet hair back out of his eyes. "Great, isn't it?"

"Do you swim every day?"

"Yes. On my bad days," he paused and made a face at her, feigning a furious frown, "I work my steam off in here."

"Then you'd better get swimming," she said as she started off sidestroking.

"I found a better way to work off my steam today," he murmured, matching his pace to hers. "The problem is," he added, pulling her to a stop and rubbing his body against hers, "my steam is rising again."

"I might be able to cool you," she murmured.

Maggie put her hands on his shoulders, leaned closer as if about to kiss him, then jumped up and dunked his head underwater before taking off with a splash. But he was quick and she shrieked as he grabbed her ankle to pull her down with him. She came up sputtering, looking around for his next attack.

"Truce," he whispered in her ear. Strong arms wrapped around her and she felt the warmth of his body against hers. "Let's go inside," he murmured, getting out of the pool and pulling her with him.

Maggie tried one last time. "Don't you have something important to work on?"

"Just you."

"But—"

"Shh." He put a finger to her lips and led her back into the bedroom. "Yes, the Trescott matter is important, but we're more important, Maggie. In order to find those missing papers we have to work together, not rip each other apart. I forgot that this morning. Can you forgive me?"

"I already have forgiven you," she whispered as he turned back the sheets and pulled her down with him. Looking into his eyes, she had the feeling she always would.

CHAPTER ELEVEN

The restaurant was dimly lighted and cozy, the seafood fresh and succulent. In fact, it was the perfect place for two lovers to dine while basking in the glow of an afternoon of sensual delight. Or almost perfect.

"Is he still staring at us?" Maggie asked.

Robert glanced casually across the crowded restaurant toward the bar. Behind the wooden lattice partition separating the dining room and lounge, a thin, well-dressed man stood watching them intently. His eyes met Robert's and he lifted his drink as if toasting the couple.

"Yes," Robert replied. "Maybe he's just overwhelmed by your charms." He took her hand and squeezed it, his voice teasing though a frown furrowed his brow. "I know I am."

Maggie suppressed an involuntary shiver. "Shouldn't we find out what he wants?"

"We'll know soon enough. He's coming over."

Looking over her shoulder, Maggie watched as the man made his way around the partition and headed in their direction. Holding onto Robert's hand for reassurance, she looked up curiously when the man arrived at their table. He was sort of handsome in an odd, overly sophisticated way, but the smug expression on his face and the intimidating way he was looking at her made Maggie take an instant dislike to him.

"May I join you?" the man asked, pulling out a chair and taking a seat without waiting for an answer.

"What the . . ." Robert stared at him, surprise mixed with anger showing on his face. "Who the hell are you?" he demanded.

"My name isn't important. I work for James Trescott." As he spoke he continued to look at Maggie. "In a way you might call me his eyes and ears. And quite frankly, Mr. Langley, I'm very concerned about what I've seen and heard lately."

"I couldn't care less what you're concerned about," Robert returned curtly. "The lady and I are having dinner and we don't wish to be disturbed. So kindly get your carcass out of that chair and—"

"Please, Mr. Langley," the man interrupted, his tone placid and expression calm. "There's no need to get belligerent." At last he turned his eyes to Robert, seemingly dismissing Maggie. Indeed, when he spoke it was as if she wasn't even there. "I'm here to help you, actually. I've discovered an interesting bit of information about your employee, disturbing information in view of the present situation with your formula."

"What are you talking about?" He glanced at Maggie. "If you're referring to Ms. Johnson, buster, you're way out of line."

The man shrugged. "Perhaps. That's why I'm here now, to find out precisely what's going on."

"James doesn't operate like this," Robert said tersely. "Does he know you're harassing us?"

"He'll know about this meeting soon enough, as well as the information I've dug up. I decided to give you the benefit of the doubt and confront you with it first."

"Confront?" Robert glared at him, muscles tense, eyes full of quiet threat. "I think you'd better make your point and make it fast."

He gazed intently at Robert, gauging his reaction as he asked, "Are you aware, Mr. Langley, that Ms. Maggie Johnson was at one time an employee of the Chapman Corporation?"

Robert's eyes widened. "What?"

"She was, in fact, Dennis Chapman's executive secretary, the very man who is shaping up to be the prime suspect in this situation with your stolen formula."

"Stolen formula?" Maggie asked. "What stolen formula?"

The thin man seemed amused. "Bravo, Maggie," he said sarcastically. "Very good. Were you an actress before you turned to industrial espionage?"

"Espionage! What on earth are you talking about?"

Robert was looking at her, confusion momentarily overriding his anger. "Did you work for Chapman?" he asked.

"It's hardly some deep, dark secret," she replied with an exasperated shrug. "I was Dennis's secretary before I signed on with Alison. He was the lousy boss I told you about, the one who was largely responsible for my decision to quit and do temporary work."

"Ms. Johnson," the man continued, "isn't it true you quit Chapman just before Marsha Lane took control of the company?"

"Well, yes, but—"

"Dennis Chapman, the founder of the company, was virtually stripped of his controlling interest and made little more than a figurehead. How did that make you feel?"

Maggie shrugged. "That's one of the dangers of going public. Dennis isn't particularly bright."

"Come now, Maggie, isn't it true you retain a sense of loyalty to Dennis Chapman?"

"No! I despise the man!"

"Isn't it true, Maggie, that when you went to work for Robert Langley you saw an opportunity to help your old boss regain control of his company, perhaps even earn yourself an executive position in that company?"

At last Robert got over his confusion, his anger coming back full force at the way the man was badgering Maggie. "Listen," he said through clenched teeth as he stood up and put his hand on the thin man's shoulder, "I've had enough of you. Get out of here before I throw you out!"

The man ignored him. "Isn't it true that you stole the face-lift formula and passed it along to Dennis Chapman, using an intermediary so as not to throw suspicion on yourself until the product could be marketed?"

"That's enough!" Robert exclaimed, the level of his voice causing the other diners to stare and the manager to come running.

"Gentlemen, please," the manager pleaded, "you'll have to quiet down or I'll be forced to ask you to leave."

"Fine," Robert replied. He grabbed Maggie's hand and hauled her from her seat. "We don't want to eat in a place that allows weasels like this in anyway."

Throwing some money on the table to cover the bill, Robert led the way out of the restaurant, Maggie on his heels with the thin man and the manager close behind. The thin man kept hurling accusations all the way out to the street.

"I said I was giving you the benefit of the doubt, Langley. I thought that maybe you were an innocent dupe, a victim. Perhaps you'd rather hear my second theory, the one I'm now convinced is the truth in light of your refusal to listen to me."

"Don't push your luck, buster," Robert warned. "I know James Trescott. He'll be appalled when I tell him about this. But losing your job is nothing compared to what'll happen to you if you don't shut up."

He continued to dog their steps out to the parking lot. "What happened, Langley? Did you get greedy, decide Trescott wasn't paying enough for your idea? Or did Chapman's agent here turn your head, make you an offer you couldn't refuse?" he taunted sarcastically.

Maggie nearly bumped into him when Robert stopped in his tracks. She could feel his muscles tense in fury, saw him clench his fists so tightly his knuckles turned white.

"Robert . . ."

"Sure," the thin man continued. "That's what happened, wasn't it? She came to work for you, talked you into double-dealing Trescott. Pretty hard package to resist. All that money and her in your bed, too, right, Langley?" He ogled Maggie. "Can't say that I blame you, but you made the wrong choice. Trescott's going to sue your socks off."

Robert turned around and faced him. "That's it. I've had all the garbage I'm going to take from you," he said, his voice barely above a whisper.

"Robert, don't. He's not worth it."

"Careful, Langley," the thin man said. "You're out of your league. I'm a combat-trained veteran."

Maggie expected a childish display of machismo and therefore turned her head when she saw Robert's hand come out of his pocket. But instead of the sounds of a fist fight all she heard was a quick, short hiss. She looked around and saw Robert helping the thin man sit down on the bumper of a nearby truck.

"It's a harmless gas," Robert told him. "Takes your breath away for a moment or two." He patted the man on the back. "With your foul mouth you have to admit you deserved it. You can insult me all you want, but don't you ever talk that way about Ms. Johnson again, understand?"

The man gasped and nodded his head. Maggie took hold of Robert's hand, so confused all she could do was stand there and watch while he defended her.

"Now you listen to me for a change," Robert said. "I don't know how Chapman got that formula, but he sure didn't get it from me or Maggie. The fact that she used to work for Dennis Chapman is a coincidence and nothing more." He looked at Maggie. Though he was frowning, he hugged her reassuringly. "So I suggest you keep digging, and tell James I'll be talking to him about this little incident tomorrow morning."

As they turned and walked arm in arm toward Robert's car, the thin man recovered enough to speak. "I was wrong, Langley," he gasped, managing to stand up. "You are a dupe. And a fool. She's conning you, can't you see that?"

This time Robert just kept walking. He opened Maggie's door for her, then slipped in beside her and started the engine. They were several blocks from the restaurant before Maggie regained her composure.

"What was that all about?" she asked.

"The Chapman Corporation has somehow managed to acquire the phase-one formula for the face-lift cream I developed and sold to Trescott Labs."

Maggie closed her eyes and nodded in understanding. "So that's what all the fuss over the missing part of the file is about."

"That's right. I need documentation to prove I developed the idea so Trescott can defend themselves and stop Chapman from coming out with the product first."

"Don't you have a patent or something?"

"A pending patent, but that's a tricky area of law at best. Chapman might be able to override my claims unless I can prove diligent workmanship, as it's called in the business—dated, witnessed log entries and such showing that the concept was mine from start to finish."

Eyes still closed, Maggie battled with the panic she felt threatening to overtake her. "And that's exactly the material we can't find."

Robert nodded. "I *know* I made those entries. I admit I'm lax about some things, but when I work on something as important as this I always keep my workshop log up to date."

"This cream . . . it's worth a lot of money, isn't it?"

"Millions."

Putting her hand on his thigh, Maggie opened her eyes and looked at him. "What happens if you can't find the papers you need?"

"It will look as if I'm holding out on them, I'm afraid. Especially in view of the fact that a former employee of Chapman now works for me." He glanced at her. "An employee they obviously know I'm involved with."

"We've been spied on?"

"Looks that way."

Maggie shivered. "What that man said, about James Trescott suing you if you can't come up with the proof . . ."

"He'll do it," Robert replied. "He has an obligation to his company and the shareholders. If they can't move against Chapman, their only alternative will be to hope for an understanding judge and use the documentation they do have: my contract signing the rights to the idea over to them."

"I'm sorry, Robert."

To her great surprise he chuckled. "For what? Working for Trescott's arch rival is hardly a crime."

"You do believe it's just a coincidence, don't you?" she asked hesitantly.

"Of course."

Robert sighed when she put her head on his shoulder. He did believe her. How could he not believe the woman he had fallen in love with? How could he not believe a woman he was fairly certain felt the same way about him? It would take more than some half-baked theories spouted by a crazy man to make him lose faith in her. A lot more.

CHAPTER TWELVE

In spite of the early morning sunshine, Maggie was sure the air in the office had taken on a blue tint. Some of the colorful epithets were hers as she continued to dig through the files for some sign of the Trescott papers. The rest were Robert's as he had a series of less-than-congenial phone conversations.

"What was that all about?" she asked when Robert abruptly hung up on someone.

"War drums," he replied ominously. "Trescott's lawyer is talking to mine, mine is talking to Chapman's, Chapman's is denying everything, and they're all starting to look at me like I'm an apple pie ready for slicing." He sat down behind his desk and breathed a loud sigh. "Will you still stand by me when I'm a penniless, has-been inventor whose ideas no manufacturing company would touch with a ten-foot pole?"

Maggie walked over to him and wrapped her arms around him from behind, kissing him tenderly on the forehead. "I'll always stand by you, Robert. But we'll beat this."

"I wish I had your optimism." He looked up at her. "Any luck?" he asked, his voice full of hope.

"Not yet. But I'll keep digging, even if I have to make a bigger mess out of this place than it was when I started working here."

Robert smiled, pulling her head down to his and kissing her soundly on the lips. "Thank you."

"It's a tall order, though," she said, indicating the small yet daunting portion of the office she still had to search. "Is there any way you can stall for time?"

"Well, for one thing I'm going to go have another talk with James, see if I can't convince him to swing his weight behind me instead of at me," he replied, standing up and kissing her again before putting on his suit coat. "I might even try to get an audience with the queen of the Chapman Corporation. She's still pretending she doesn't have the slightest idea what's happening."

"Good luck," Maggie told him, hugging him affectionately.

"You too."

After she watched him leave in his car, Maggie once again faced the files. "It's you or me, guys," she muttered. "And I take no prisoners."

She simply had to find the rest of that file. The man she loved was about to enter into legal battle virtually unarmed, and she saw it as her duty to get to the bottom of this mystery. She smiled as she worked despite the frustration she felt.

Maggie didn't know exactly when it had happened. It was entirely possible the process had begun the moment their eyes had met. Whenever it had happened, thunderbolts and bells aside, she was totally, hopelessly in love with Robert. Her feelings for him brought home the urgency of this situation. She simply had to save him, and no one was better equipped for the task.

Disorganization, after all, was the culprit here. As Robert had said, files didn't sprout legs and walk away. Organization was her business, so all she had to do was her job, the one she'd been hired for, the one Robert was counting on her to perform.

Out of habit she paused for lunch, hoping that somewhere Robert was doing the same, but knowing full well he probably had no more appetite than she did. Her sandwich lay on the desk untouched as she perused one of Robert's old workshop notebooks.

Every now and then, she noticed, Robert had signed and dated one of the pages. She also noticed that as a project neared completion, he had gotten somebody else to sign the log as well, witnessing what he had referred to as his diligent workmanship. This was the kind of dated material missing from the Trescott file.

She saw that Robert's sister had been called upon to perform the task quite a few times, as well as Ted Myers, the maintenance man. Maggie also recognized the cramped hand of Robert's former, faint-hearted secretary.

"Wait a minute," she mumbled, peering closely at the odd collection of drawings and specifications. "What have we here?"

The signature of somebody named Craig Smith started appearing regularly in Robert's logs. While the other witnesses seemed to be whoever was on hand at the time, Craig Smith was evidently working with Robert. Some of the day-to-day entries even appeared to have been made in his easily recognizable handwriting. But who was he?

Then Maggie remembered Robert mentioning a former assistant. If he had been working so closely with Craig Smith, however, why hadn't Robert talked about him more? It puzzled her, so she went to the file cabinet and pulled out the personnel records, finding no mention of Craig Smith. Nor did his name appear on any of the payroll ledgers. It was as if the man had never even worked there.

Maggie felt her heart skip a beat. Files didn't walk away by themselves, but they could certainly be carried away by someone who had access to them, who knew just what to take to make it impossible for Robert to prove his ownership of the face-lift cream. Someone like Craig Smith.

Then again, if there was reason to suspect him, why hadn't his name come up before now? It was obvious Robert didn't think Craig Smith had anything to do with the theft of the formula; he'd hardly even mentioned the man.

"That's it!" Maggie exclaimed, snapping her fingers as a flash of insight hit her.

Craig Smith hadn't been erased from the filing system, she realized; he'd never been there in the first place. Meticulous with some things, Robert had a tendency to be eccentrically lax with others —especially those he didn't deem important enough to be concerned about. It was obvious his former assistant fell into the latter category.

If copying someone was the sincerest form of flattery, ignoring them was the sincerest form of contempt. Evidently Robert didn't think enough of Craig Smith to keep records of their association or even consider him a threat. Contempt, indeed, and possibly a dangerous assumption.

But how could she prove her theory? The answer seemed obvious to Maggie: confront the man and see what happened. Of course, she would have to find him before she could confront him, and the urgency of the situation made it imperative she do so quickly—and therefore alone.

Robert was busy doing his part, stalling for time and trying to keep his head off the chopping block. Maggie would have to do hers and give James Trescott somebody else to go after with his legal ax.

"Death and taxes," she murmured as she picked up the phone and dialed the number of Robert's accountant.

There might not be any record of Craig's employment in the office, but even if Robert disliked him he would have to have gotten paid sometime. The government took a dim view of money changing hands without their knowing about it, and accountants had a penchant for staying on the right side of the Internal Revenue Service.

"Hello, this is Maggie Johnson from Robert Langley's office. We've misplaced the address for a former employee of ours named Craig Smith. Do you have a copy of his last withholding statement?"

Robert's temper was near the boiling point. He'd wasted the morning trying to get in to see Chapman's reigning dictator, Marsha Lane. After waiting until almost one, he had been politely but firmly escorted from the building by a security guard who kept telling him they had no need for any new cosmetic inventions at this time.

Trescott Labs had been somewhat more congenial, allowing him to have lunch in their cafeteria —he'd barely picked at the meal—while they decided whether or not it was a good idea to talk to a man they were about to sue for breach of contract.

Several times during the day Robert had picked up the phone to call Maggie, as much for her moral support as to see if she'd found anything yet. But he decided that bothering her every five minutes wouldn't help her do her job and might even make her so frantic she'd overlook something. Besides, he was mad at the whole world and hardly a fit person to talk to anyway.

Now, however, as he watched evening close in while waiting alone in James Trescott's office, Robert decided he'd better call Maggie for an update. It didn't help his mood at all when he got no answer at the workshop or her home. Where could she be?

The office door opened behind him and he spun around expectantly, his expression turning glacial when he saw the thin man from the restaurant last night enter right behind James Trescott.

"I appreciate your seeing me, James, but did you have to bring your henchman along?" Robert asked sarcastically, fixing the man with a belligerent glare.

"Take it easy, Robert," James replied. "I'm not fond of his methods either, but I'm a survivor and he's proven useful on numerous occasions. In fact, this time he may have even saved *your* bacon."

"What?"

"That's right, Mr. Langley. I think we're getting close to figuring this out," the man said. "I apologize for getting a bit overzealous last night, but I'm good at my job and that happens sometimes." He extended his hand. "No hard feelings?"

Robert kept his hands at his sides. "You've got to be kidding. And if your solution includes Maggie—"

"Maybe it does and maybe it doesn't. Either way you won't get the jump on me again, Langley," the thin man said, though he was keeping his distance.

"Gentlemen, please," James interjected impatiently. "If you insist on hating each other do so in the privacy of your thoughts. We have work to do." He took a seat, indicating that they should do the same, and opened the file folder he had carried in with him. "Do you recognize these two men, Robert?" he asked, pushing a photograph across the desk.

Robert looked at the black-and-white picture. He shrugged. "Sure. That's Dennis Chapman," he said, pointing to one of the men, "and the other is Craig Smith."

James looked at the thin man, who nodded and told him, "That's the name we have on him, too, sir." He turned from his employer and gazed intently at Robert. "Would you mind telling us how you know Mr. Smith?"

Robert shrugged again and leaned back in his chair. "He's a former assistant of mine. The relationship didn't work out and I sent him on his way. Why?"

"One of my operatives has been tailing Mr. Smith. This photo was taken during one of the many clandestine meetings he and Dennis Chapman have had over the past few days."

"So? Craig's an inventor, too, though I use the term loosely. He's not particularly bright or what you'd call successful, but I suppose it's remotely possible he came up with something an equally dim bulb like Chapman might find interesting."

"Robert," James said, "it looks like Smith and Chapman are behind this whole thing. Without the knowledge of anyone at the Chapman Corpora-

214

tion, Dennis has evidently entered into a contractual relationship with Craig Smith."

Robert frowned. "What?"

"It's simple, Mr. Langley," the other man said with an impatient sigh. "This Smith character has sold the formula for the face-lift cream—your formula—to Chapman and is helping him get ready to produce it behind the rest of the company's back," he explained. "I assume Chapman hopes to regain control of his firm by showing how brilliant he is, making millions off one product while his rival Marsha Lane is piddling along with hair spray."

"He'll lose even his figurehead status if I have anything to say about it," James grumbled. "And maybe his thieving hide as well."

"Wait a minute. . . ." Robert chuckled in spite of the others' serious expressions. "Are you asking me to believe that Craig stole the formula?" He shook his head, laughing openly now. "No way. I fired the man because he was a plodding, unimaginative, and totally incompetent nitwit. He couldn't even recognize a saleable idea, let alone steal it."

"Nevertheless—"

"And even if he did," Robert continued, the trace of a frown intruding on his amusement, "he couldn't just trot off and sell it to Chapman. As a condition to my taking him on, I had him sign a disclaimer waiving all rights to any project he worked on with me or became aware of through contact with me or my notes."

"A document that I assume is in the same file as the ones you've so conveniently lost, Robert?" James asked.

Robert's expression turned sober. He wasn't laughing now. "I don't know," he replied honestly. "I haven't seen it since . . ."

"Since Maggie Johnson came to work for you?" the thin man completed in a smug voice.

"No!" He turned and glared at him. "I told you to watch your mouth where Maggie is concerned. She's searching for the papers right now and when she finds them I'm going to ram them right—"

"Stop it, both of you," James demanded curtly. "It's obvious we don't know the whole story, so it's pointless to second-guess. No one is accusing Maggie of anything, Robert."

"Yet," the thin man added vindictively.

Robert started to get up, but the phone rang, forestalling any retribution. James handed it to his sneering henchman, who had a quick conversation, then hung up with a speculative frown on his gaunt face.

"That was the operative who's been sticking close to Smith. She said he's heading for another meeting."

"With Chapman?" James wanted to know.

"She's not sure, but she doesn't think so. He was bragging about making another killing and how he might be able to buy her a mink sooner than he'd expected."

"Is she following?"

He shook his head. "Another of my people is on his tail. He'll contact me when Smith arrives at his destination, which I'm sure will be the same place he always uses for these little tête-à-têtes," he replied, glancing at Robert. "You're right about one thing, Langley. Smith doesn't have much of an imagination. He's taken to meeting Chapman in a dark alley near the old industrial section. Guy thinks he's Sam Spade."

"Efficient slime, aren't you?" Robert observed caustically.

"Anytime you're ready to see how efficient, hotshot, you just let me know," the man countered.

James Trescott stopped them this time by standing up decisively. "I think we should go have a talk with Craig Smith, and Chapman too if he's there," he said, striding toward the door. "Come on, I'll have my secretary pass your operative's call along to my car phone, and meanwhile we'll head for that side of town. Tag along, Robert. I want to see what Craig Smith has to say to you."

"Let's go," the thin man said, following his boss with an eagerness that made Robert frown.

"I'll be with you in a second," he told them. "I'm going to check in with Maggie."

When they'd left, Robert dialed his workshop and Maggie's house, once again getting no answer at either place. His frown deepened. Here he was, battling for his professional life, and she was off gallivanting. It wasn't like her. The worry on his face evident, he went to join the other two men by the elevator.

"Has she come up with anything yet?" James asked.

Robert shook his head. "I can't get hold of her. She must be in transit."

"I'll just bet she is," the thin man remarked quietly, his expression thoughtful.

As she drove to her meeting with Craig Smith, Maggie congratulated herself again for a job well done. She felt like a detective hot on the trail of a suspect, and was even dressed like one, having convinced herself that it looked enough like rain to wear a stylish wide-brimmed hat and raincoat without appearing overly dramatic.

Robert's accountant had indeed had an address for Craig Smith, and a quick call to the operator had produced a phone number. But she couldn't just call and accuse him, nor could she arrange a meeting without gaining his interest in some way. That was when she had a stroke of genius. Her plan made him agree so readily to see her she knew without doubt he was guilty.

Craig Smith had taken the phase-one formula. What better bait to tempt him with than the work Robert had done thus far on phase two? Smith was leery, naturally, but he was greedy, too, and by convincing him she was just as greedy, Maggie had arranged to meet him at a place of his choosing.

She wasn't too happy about his choice, though.

As she turned down the nearly deserted street she briefly wondered where all the people were, then realized they were all on the freeways heading home; she had battled traffic all the way there. At least she wouldn't have any trouble finding a parking place.

This section of town was strictly industrial, near the river on the outskirts of downtown, gloomy, dirty, and void of activity at this hour save those poor souls working overtime. Maggie pulled into the empty parking lot of a photographic laboratory, got out of her car, and walked toward the end of the street. Ahead of her through the gathering gloom streetlights illuminated her destination, a rather pathetic-looking swatch of grass masquerading as a park.

It was amazingly quiet. She could hear the freeway traffic in the distance, as well as the hollow, mechanical noise of air conditioners operating atop the nearby buildings. But on this isolated street the predominant sound was that of her high heels clicking on the pavement as she approached the entrance to the park. Trees spread their branches over the pathway, deepening the shadows and lending a mysterious quality to the scene. It started to drizzle.

"Here's looking at you, sweetheart," Maggie muttered through clenched teeth in her best impression of Humphrey Bogart.

She took a final look over her shoulder. The only other car in sight was a black Lincoln Continental parked in front of the last building on the block, its tinted windows preventing her from seeing inside. Craig Smith's car? Probably, and purchased with his ill-gotten gains from stealing Robert's formula no doubt. The thought strengthened her resolve and Maggie continued on her way.

"What do you have to say about your loyal secretary now, hotshot?" the thin man asked Robert.

Looking out the window of the black Lincoln, Robert watched as Maggie strode purposefully into the park at the end of the street. He refused to believe his eyes. There had to be a reasonable explanation.

"Maybe she figured out that Craig was the one behind all this and decided to confront him," he replied with a certainty belying his inner turmoil.

"Perhaps," James Trescott said, his tone doubtful. "You did say she was an enterprising and resourceful woman."

The industrial spy chuckled. "She's enterprising all right. I wonder which of your ideas she's selling Smith now."

"Quit gloating. I'm sure he feels bad enough as it is," James ordered curtly.

"Why should I feel bad?" Robert objected. "So she's meeting with Craig, so what? We don't know what's going on. There are a lot of explanations for this." He just wished he could think of one that made any sense.

"We'll know soon enough," the thin man said.

"There's Smith." He lifted an odd device he held cradled in his lap and pointed it through the windshield toward the park. Suddenly the sounds of Maggie's footsteps filled the interior of the car, coming from an amplified speaker on the seat beside him. "Listen up, Langley. You're about to hear the proof with your own two ears."

James Trescott shifted uncomfortably. "I hate this."

"Me too," Robert mumbled. He leaned forward and peered through the drizzle at the two people standing in the park. "Turn up the volume."

Maggie tensed and tried not to gasp. The man seemed to simply appear in front of her, slipping from the shadows at the edge of the sidewalk and blocking her path.

Though barely into his forties, Craig Smith's hair was gray, or at least the few thin strands of it he had left were gray. His face showed signs of premature aging as well, with deep furrows etched into his shallow forehead and what looked to be a permanently sour expression on his face. His eyes, a washed-out blue, seemed full of disappointment and tinged with hatred for everybody and everything around him. He smiled, and Maggie had the feeling it was at a particularly evil joke only he understood.

"C-Craig?" she stuttered. Why it hadn't occurred to her that this meeting could be dangerous she'd never know. She cursed herself and tried to look relaxed. "Nice night, isn't it?"

Craig Smith's smile disappeared at her flip tone. He had hoped to start the negotiations for Langley's second-phase formula from a position of strength, such as with this Johnson woman scared of him. But she seemed surprisingly calm under the circumstances, so he decided to take another approach.

"Good weather if you're a duck," he replied, smiling again. "It's Maggie, right?" She nodded. "We might as well be sociable if we're going to do business."

Maggie didn't like him. He was an odd little man, nearly a foot shorter than she was, with an evil sort of smile that made her shiver though the drizzle falling around them was the warm spring variety. He was trying to get chummy, and she decided to put a stop to that immediately.

"On the phone you said you'd bring proof you're the one who appropriated the phase-one formula," she said briskly. "I want to know I'm dealing with the right man."

"And you said you would have the preliminary formula for phase two," he replied just as briskly. "Let's trade."

Maggie slipped a file folder from beneath her raincoat. Craig pulled an envelope out of his pocket. He was wearing a trench coat no less, and the incongruous thought occurred to her that they probably looked like two secret agents exchanging classified documents.

She tried not to show her excitement as she looked at the contents of Craig's envelope. It was a contract with the Chapman Corporation assigning them the rights to what was described as a chemical face-lift cream, signed by none other than her former boss, Dennis Chapman. She had ferreted out both the culprit and his contact at Chapman. Robert was going to be so proud of her!

"I was under the impression Dennis no longer had the authority to purchase products for Chapman," she said, managing to sound skeptical.

"You used to be his secretary," Craig murmured in a distracted tone as he perused the contents of the file folder. "You know he has his own resources. He's using them to unseat Marsha Lane and take control of the company again."

"I see." So that was why the rest of the Chapman Corporation didn't know what was going on.

"This is pretty thin," Craig said, flicking the folder with his finger disdainfully. "Where are the particulars?"

Maggie chuckled in what she hoped was a show of calm bravado. "Come on now, Craig. You expected me to bring them to our first meeting?"

"Pretty sharp cookie, aren't you?"

"Sharp enough to cut myself in on a piece of the action."

"And if I just tell you to buzz off?"

"Then you don't get phase two, or any of the

other ideas I can pilfer from Langley's files before Trescott shuts him down," she told him, playing the tough. "I've got an inside track with Langley. You have Dennis Chapman's ear. Of course, I could always prove my loyalty to the company and go talk with good old Dennis myself."

"All right," Craig said quickly. "A sixty-forty split on whatever you can bring me. When can we meet again to finish the deal on the phase-two formula?"

"Not so fast. We go halves. And the next time we meet at my place where we won't get our feet wet." And where she would have Robert, James Trescott, and maybe even Marsha Lane on hand to nab this little weasel.

Craig deliberated for a moment before nodding his head decisively. "All right. You give me a call, but make it soon. Langley's going down the road to ruin faster than I dared hope."

"What do you mean?"

"Chapman's all set. They start production on phase one in a few more weeks and Trescott will lop off Langley's head shortly thereafter."

"There's no sign of the proof he needs to reclaim the idea, that's for sure," she said in a friendly, conversational tone. "He's had me digging through that mare's nest of an office of his for days."

Craig laughed derisively. "I knew he wouldn't have the slightest idea what happened to the stuff. His disorganization was what gave me the idea to rip him off in the first place," he told her. "Don't strain your eyes looking, Maggie. It's gone, all of it, burned to ashes long ago. He can never prove the idea for the cream was his now, and soon it won't matter one way or the other. You and I will have jobs at Chapman and the last laugh on Robert Langley."

"Well. I guess that's that," James Trescott said sadly, depression hovering around him like a cloud.

"Tough break, Langley," the thin man agreed.

Robert was staring numbly out the car window, not really seeing the two people who had betrayed him. "All that work," he mumbled. "My idea . . ."

"At least you can console yourself with the fact that Maggie wasn't in on this from the beginning," James said. He looked at Robert, not liking himself one bit for what he had to say to the inventor now. "Your proof is gone, Robert. There's no way we can get control of the cream now. You have to understand, the board . . . I'm going to have to bring suit against you for breach of contract. The firm will have to be reimbursed for the research money it put out."

Robert barely heard him. What did it matter if they sued him? What did it matter that afterward he wouldn't have a snowball's chance in hell of selling another idea? The woman he loved had sold him out, was using his trust in her to help destroy him. Nothing mattered except the pain he felt inside.

"She's leaving," the thin man noted.

His eyes focusing again, Robert watched as Maggie walked down the street toward her car. Suddenly feeling a raging anger blot out his despair, he grabbed the door handle and started to get out of the car.

"Don't do it, Langley. She's not worth it."

"Let him go."

As he walked toward her, Robert cursed himself for still feeling the usual pang inside at her beauty. But he had to confront her, make her see the anguish her betrayal was causing him, and find out if she had even the slightest remorse.

When the door to the big, black car opened, Maggie thought her heart would stop. She saw the man approaching her, unrecognizable through the rain yet somehow familiar.

"Robert!" she cried in surprise when he was close enough to see clearly. She took a step toward him, then stopped when she noticed the furious scowl on his face. "What—"

"Shut up!" he said viciously. "I don't want to hear any of your denials. We heard the whole thing." He jerked his thumb over his shoulder, indicating the car and the men inside watching through the open window.

She recognized the man who had accosted them in the restaurant. The other was unfamiliar. "I don't understand."

"That's James Trescott, the man who is going to have to ruin me thanks to your new partner."

"But I wasn't—"

"What happened, Maggie?" he interrupted, grabbing her by the shoulders. "Did you decide that as long as I was being ruined you might as well make a profit? Or did you have something like this in mind all along, and Craig just showed up to make your job easier?"

"No!" She knew he was in pain, could see it in his eyes, but that didn't make her any less angry at his accusations and the way he refused to listen to her. "I don't know what you're talking about! I figured out it was Craig who stole the phase-one formula and tracked him down. I set up this meeting with him to—"

Robert shook her roughly. "Stop! I heard it all, remember? You set up the meeting to cut yourself in on a piece of the action." He pulled her coat open and took the file folder from her. "Well, you can think again. Nobody will buy this after Trescott finishes with me. But I'll be damned if I'll let you and that scum take it from me."

"Don't be so stupid, Robert!" Tears welled in her eyes and rolled down her cheeks at the pain his words caused her. "I wasn't stealing anything from you. I was trying to get to the bottom of this. I contacted Craig and used the file as bait. Next time we met I was going to have everybody there to catch him in the act," she said, her words tumbling over each other in her effort to explain. "We can still do it. We can get Chapman to stop. Marsha Lane will hang them both by the thumbs."

"Now you're being stupid!" Robert yelled. "Once that product hits the market Marsha Lane will be out of a job. And even if she isn't she'll know a good thing when she sees it. I can't stop them, your buddy Craig saw to that." He shook her again, then released her. "Don't worry. You picked the right side. I'm sure Dennis will hire you back when he finds out how loyal you are to his company."

"Loyal! You wouldn't know loyalty if it came up and bit you on the leg, Robert Langley. I'm loyal to *you*. I wouldn't steal from you. I—"

"Don't say it," he warned, his voice barely above a whisper now. "You're not worming your way back into my life so you can pilfer my files again. It's over, Maggie."

The Lincoln pulled up beside him and the door swung open. "Come on, Robert," James said forlornly. "The least I can do is give you a ride."

"You see?" Robert said. "This man has to take me apart brick by professional brick, but at least he'll do it with style. Admit defeat and go away, Maggie." Seeing the look of anguish on her face, Robert felt his heart break. Hurting her hadn't helped his own pain at all. "You know the worst part? I didn't just fall for your line. I fell for you too."

"Robert—"

"I told you, Maggie. Just go away."

Maggie stood there and watched him get into the car, wincing as he slammed the door. She was stunned into silence, knowing that he wouldn't listen even if she could speak. Her dream, the pleasant world of a future with Robert, was falling to pieces right before her eyes.

James Trescott's industrial spy rolled down the window and looked at Maggie appraisingly. "Hey," the thin man said, "if you need a job, come see me. I think I might be able to use a woman of your talents." Then the long black car roared off, leaving her standing in the rain totally alone.

CHAPTER THIRTEEN

At first all Maggie could think about was the pain of her broken heart. Then, slowly, her anger took over and she began planning retribution. Should she burn all his files? Go to his house and put dye in the water of his pool so that the next time he swam he'd turn as blue as she felt?

Once she calmed down, however, she knew exactly what she was going to do. Trying to get back at him for accusing her unjustly was not only childish, it was pointless. Unless someone helped Robert out of this mess, he would be ruined anyway. Maggie didn't want that to happen.

In spite of the way he had behaved, she loved Robert, and knew deep inside that she always would. He may have lost faith in her, but she still had faith in him—and his abilities. She was still angry, too, but they could argue later. Right now she had to help him.

Trescott Labs was easy to find; getting into the building at night was not, but she was determined. She was positive James Trescott would be in his office, mulling over the problem. Maggie had to talk to him, convince him that there was another option open to him besides ruining the man she loved.

"I'm telling you, Mr. Trescott knows me," she told the security guard who confronted her the moment she walked through the door. "Ring his office and tell him I'm here."

The guard continued to look at her doubtfully, then at last decided to confer with a higher authority. "You just stay right there until the head of security gets here," he ordered, cutting her off before she could begin anew.

Maggie did as she was told, tapping her foot impatiently. Having worked for security-conscious companies before, she knew she would have to work her way through the hierarchy. Dealing with the status quo didn't help her temper any; she wanted to burst forth with her arguments right now, before she cooled off.

The head of security arrived at last. "What's the problem?" he asked, eyeing her suspiciously.

Maggie sighed. "Oh, for heaven's sake. See?" she asked, turning around with her arms held in the air. "No guns or bombs." This man was twice the size of the other and looked like an ex-boxer. Would they just keep getting bigger and meaner the farther into the building she got? "I want to see James Trescott and I want to see him now," she demanded.

As if he didn't even trust her enough to say it

properly, the other guard repeated her request. "This lady says she knows the boss and wants to speak to him."

"What's her name?"

"Maggie Johnson," Maggie said impatiently.

"Maggie Johnson," the guard repeated.

The big man closed his eyes and sighed. "Okay. I'll handle this, you continue your rounds," he told the other man. He turned his attention to Maggie. "Come with me, ma'am."

Maggie followed him. His voice was surprisingly soft, not intimidating at all. "Is security always this tight?" she asked, waiting for him to unlock a door.

He gave her an assessing look. "No. Most of the time it's better." He held the door open for her. "You should have been stopped at the front gate," he replied as he locked the door behind him. "Why weren't you?"

"Just lucky, I guess." Now was not the time to tell him she had parked outside the main gate and slipped by the guardhouse on foot.

They walked down a spacious hallway, their footsteps making a hollow echo. Dim lights were spaced evenly along the fiber-textured walls to illuminate their way. She followed the big man to a phone near the elevators and waited impatiently while he made the required call.

"James, this is Charlie. I have Langley's secretary down here. She's quite anxious to see you." He glanced at her. "No, I don't know how she got on the grounds. Okay, we'll be right up." They stepped into the elevator.

"How did you know—"

"I'm kept well informed, especially about potential troublemakers. You're involved with Robert Langley and we're having problems with him," he explained. The elevator stopped its upward climb and he guided her out. "You're not going to cause us problems, are you?"

"Not in the way you mean, no."

"Good."

"Do you know Robert?"

"Yes."

"Then you must know he's not a troublemaker either."

"Ms. Johnson, what you or I or anyone else believes doesn't matter at this point. Facts are facts. Robert allowed this to happen and he'll have to accept the consequences." He unlocked another door. "After you," he said, indicating still another door.

The room she entered was well lighted and smelled of fresh coffee. James Trescott was present, as well as the jerk who spied on innocent people, and another man she hadn't expected to see.

"Hello, Maggie," Colt greeted her softly.

"Colt." She nodded to him, then looked at the head of the company. "Mr. Trescott." She ignored the jerk.

"How did she get in?"

Charlie looked at Maggie. "Well?"

"I walked in," she replied with a self-satisfied smile.

Charlie was already out the door. "I'm checking on it."

Maggie looked at the three men who stared back at her and decided to get right to the point. "You know Robert didn't give away or sell the formula, correct?" She looked at James Trescott, her eyes not wavering from his. "Don't you?" she pressed.

"Yes."

"And you also know there are ways around this problem?"

"Ms. Johnson, I do not intend to discuss—"

"Let's hear her out, James," Colt interrupted. "There's too much at stake here not to." He looked at her, a small, speculative smile tugging at the corners of his mouth. "Have a seat, Maggie Johnson."

"No, thank you." Her nervousness would then become apparent to all; she was too wound up to sit still.

"Well?" the thin man prompted with a patronizing sneer.

"We all know Robert would never get around to filing the necessary papers for a patent himself. He was smart enough—and successful enough—to hire an attorney who makes out his applications for new patents and who keeps track of the old ones."

"So?" James asked.

"So even though his memory of such mundane

234

matters does tend to bear a strong resemblance to a sieve, Robert is also smart enough to keep copies of other important documents with his lawyer as well."

"Such as?"

"Such as employee waivers of ownership to his ideas."

James's eyebrows arched. "Are you sure?"

"Positive. Though I'm sure he forgot telling me to do so, he had me bring my waiver to his lawyer the day I started."

"You're kidding," James interrupted. "You could have just thrown the thing away."

Maggie smiled. "True. But I didn't."

"I'm sure Craig wasn't as honest," the thin man pointed out in a sarcastic tone.

Maggie did her best not to kick the jerk in the shins. "He did destroy the original, I'm sure. But somehow or other—sheer luck, probably—a copy of Craig's agreement is in Robert's lawyer's office."

"I admire your ability to get such information out of a lawyer at this time of night, Ms. Johnson, but I'm afraid it doesn't make any difference," Trescott informed her. "Without the logs and the other material we know for a fact has been destroyed, we can't corroborate Robert's claim of ownership in the first place."

"But you can prove that the man who sold the formula to Chapman did in fact work for Robert right before Robert filed for a patent on that formula."

"That doesn't prove anything," the thin man interjected in his irritating, sarcastic tone. "Craig can claim he was the one who invented the stuff and that Langley stole the idea from him."

"But did he file for a patent?"

"It doesn't matter," Colt said, joining the conversation for the first time. "Patent law is a tricky arena, Maggie."

"You mean it doesn't make a difference who files first?"

"Not always. It's documentation that makes the difference in a case like this—signed, dated proof."

"But Robert's proof was stolen, and—"

"And we'd need proof of that, too," James told her. He paused, looking straight at her. "And Robert doesn't have it, does he?"

"No."

"Neither do we." Trescott rubbed his tired eyes with the back of his hands. "You see, Maggie, the truth of the matter is that Chapman has the formula and they'd be foolish not to produce this product. And even if we had the proof we needed to win in court, these cases are expensive and drag on forever."

This discussion wasn't going the way she had thought it would. "Well, then, if the patent's so shaky and you both have the formula, why don't you produce it too?"

James shook his head wearily. "If we both bring the product out at the same time, it cuts our yield in half."

"Then do it first!" Maggie cried.

Colt chuckled at her emotional outburst. "We'd still be going head to head with our competition. And even if it's not true, they have proof that their inventor came up with the product first. Chapman would simply come out with an announcement the next day, touting a superior product."

"So much for the easy way out," she mumbled.

"Why don't you just face it, lady?" the thin man asked with a shrug. "There's nothing you can do to save the man. Let him bite the bullet. Now, about that job I offered you."

Maggie turned on him and glared. "Listen, you—"

The phone rang, and James held up his hand to cut her off. "Trescott."

Taking the opportunity the interruption provided him, Colt stood up and walked over to the door. He opened it and looked at the thin man. "We won't be needing you anymore this evening."

He shrugged. "Suits me."

Maggie watched as he got up and left the room, feeling better the instant Colt closed the door behind him. She couldn't help it if she despised the man for the type of work he did, necessary or not.

"Now, I believe you were about to make yet another bid for Robert, Maggie?" James asked as he replaced the phone receiver on its cradle.

She was, but she was grasping at straws and she knew it. Still, nothing else seemed to be getting through to them, so she had to give it a try.

"What if he improved the product?"

"How?"

"Made it work faster, last longer." Maggie gestured uncertainly. "I'm not sure."

James cleared his throat. "We don't have the time."

"You said the rival firm just got their hands on the formula last week," she objected. "If that's correct, then they can't possibly have tested or geared up for production."

"We've been testing this product for almost six months," James informed her. "Just because we feel a responsibility to the public doesn't mean they do." He shook his head negatively. "Our reputation is on the line."

"Didn't Craig Smith steal the original formula, with the cheaper ingredients Robert started with?"

"Yes."

"He said the formula wouldn't work that way, that—"

"Correction," Colt interjected. "It will work, but not very effectively."

Maggie frowned. She was onto something, but couldn't figure out what it was. "Some of the ingredients were changed after he applied for the application and the other company doesn't know about those changes unless you've had a security leak."

"True."

"And what about the one expensive ingredient Robert wanted to add and you vetoed?"

James Trescott let his calm mask slip a little at this revelation. "How do you know about that?" he demanded.

Maggie smiled. She had actually gotten a reaction out of the man. He had the type of face that gave no indication of what he was really thinking —until now—and it had been very disconcerting.

"I wasn't spying, if that's what you mean," she retorted. "I'm his secretary, remember? I found a note in the trash can, alongside his canceled checks."

Colt cracked a smile at the picture she painted. "I see Robert hasn't changed his filing system."

Trescott was shaking his head negatively. "The reason we vetoed that ingredient was that it will increase the cost 20 to 40 percent."

"But you did test it?"

"Yes." James looked into her angry, flashing eyes. The woman had guts. It had been a long time since someone had dared to talk to him this way, and he admired her for her courage. "Though the results weren't consistent enough to justify the cost."

"But if Robert could work with it, make the face-lifting effect last longer, with better results, then . . ." Maggie's words trailed off as she finally saw the light. "You don't want to put out a better product!" she accused. "You want one they'll have to buy more often so you can get even more of their money!"

"Now you listen to—"

"No. You listen to me!" she cried, pounding her fists down on his desk. "Robert Langley is fighting for his livelihood here and you are damn well going to give him a chance! He came to this company in good faith. He gave you the opportunity to produce his idea. Well? Didn't he?"

"Yes," he replied calmly.

Maggie paced around the room, barely able to contain her outrage. "He's already improved the original product he supplied to you and he can do it again."

"Probably."

"But he can't do it unless you give him the chance," she continued heatedly. "Who cares if it costs more?"

"We do. And the consumer does," James replied in a calm, reasonable voice. For some reason he was smiling and looking at Colt.

"If it works people will be more than willing to pay whatever price you ask. And Chapman can say whatever they like about coming up with the idea first or having a superior product," Maggie told him. "If you have a cream that works better and lasts longer, people will buy yours every time. Don't you realize that?"

James continued to smile, not saying a word. He was still looking at Colt, who was chuckling heartily. Maggie fixed them with a suspicious glare.

"What's so funny?"

"Not a thing," Colt managed to say.

"And you!" Maggie cried, facing the enigmatic

stockholder squarely. "I thought you were his friend, Colt. Why aren't you helping me?"

"You don't need any help."

Trescott started laughing. "He's on your side."

"You are?" Colt nodded. "Then why—"

"You said it all, and much more emotionally than I ever could."

Maggie collapsed in a chair against the wall, completely drained. She had given it her best shot and the rest was up to someone else. "I hate men," she muttered.

They ignored her mumbled epithets. "Then you agree, James?" Colt asked.

"Yes, Maggie convinced me. But it's your job to convince the other board members."

Maggie looked from one to the other, her eyes narrowing. "You had already decided before I got here?" she asked James.

"No. Colt was just starting in on me when you arrived and took over for him." He grinned. "I must admit I'd rather be yelled at by you any day, Maggie."

"Come on, Maggie, I'll walk you to your car," Colt offered, pulling her out of the chair.

"But—"

"Calm down. You've won Robert a second chance," Colt told her, ushering her out of the room and into an elevator. "But you need to learn to quit while you're still ahead. Wait here." Colt walked over to the wall phone and punched in a number. "Charlie, Ms. Johnson is leaving now and I'll be lifting off soon."

"I have to find Robert," she said on the elevator ride down. "He has to be told and—"

"I'll find him and let him know what he has to do."

"You believe he can do it, don't you?"

Colt tipped back his head and laughed. "If he managed to win the loyalty of a woman like you, Maggie Johnson, I firmly believe Robert can do anything. Now go home and get some sleep."

CHAPTER FOURTEEN

Robert had every right to feel claustrophobic. The world was literally closing in on him, pressing at him from all sides. The impending collapse of his career was like a strangling cloud around him, Maggie's betrayal an unbearable weight on his heart and soul. Though he had all the windows of his car open as he roared down the highway, he still felt as if he couldn't breathe.

He had to have open space, with nothing over his head but the night sky and twinkling stars. Without stopping to think of the agony the memory would cause him, he headed for the seclusion of Colt's ranch. But the moment he stepped out of the car it hit him, came back in a rush of remembered emotions and sensations.

The picnic. The taste of Maggie's sun-warmed skin under his lips, her intoxicating fragrance, her happy laughter as he chased her around the tree. If he closed his eyes he could almost feel the softness of her breasts against his cheek. How could it be over? His love for her still burned within him, seemed etched upon every fiber of his being.

This whole situation was a nightmare, nothing more. When he opened his eyes he would awaken and Maggie would be here with him, smiling at him, making the crushing weight of this bad dream disappear. But when his eyelids fluttered open he knew what a fool he was. She was gone. He had told her to go. It was over.

The sky over the field in which he stood remained clear, though thunder rolled in the distance. He could smell the approaching rain, feel the humidity on his skin as a soft breeze whirled the night air around him.

Looking up, Robert tried to draw comfort from the eternal, brightly winking stars. He was but a speck, a dust mote, his problems as fleeting as the tick of a clock in the grand design of time.

"If this is love's design," he muttered to himself, "then I want to have a word with the inventor."

His eyes widened when one of the stars detached itself from the rest and started descending on the field. For a moment his confused mind thought his request for an audience with Eros had been granted, then he heard a chopping sound and felt a sudden rush of air on his face.

The helicopter settled to earth, landing lights flashing and cutting intermittent swaths through the darkness. A man got out, ducking beneath the slowing rotor as he came toward Robert with a long-legged stride. His expression was as unfathomable as ever, the short scar on his face nearly invisible in the dim light of the moon.

"Thought I'd find you here, Robert," Colt drawled as he stopped in front of him. "Are you out here trying to get hit by lightning?"

"It's not a bad idea."

Colt thrust his hands into the pockets of his jeans and leaned back to join his friend's perusal of the night sky. "We're going to get wet in a few minutes."

Robert turned and looked at the hard, black-haired man standing beside him. "Did you come out here just to tell me that, Colt?" he asked. "Or were you and Trescott worried I'd disappear and cheat you out of the public execution you have planned?"

"Robert," he replied placidly, "for such an intelligent man, you can be the dumbest jackass I've ever known."

"Thanks, buddy." Robert turned and looked at him angrily. "Do you want me to hold the bag of salt while you rub it in my wound?"

Colt chuckled. "Tell you what. I'll hold the salt while you rub it in. I wouldn't want to deprive you of the opportunity to wallow in some more self-pity. Or maybe we should just get right to it and have the knockdown, drag-out fight you seem to be looking for."

"I'm not wallowing in self-pity," Robert objected. He saw the arch of Colt's brow and laughed in spite of himself. "Okay, so maybe I am dipping my feet in a bit, but I'm not wallowing."

"Could have fooled me."

"You still want that fight?"

Colt looked sorely tempted, his piercing green eyes meeting Robert's defiant gaze with something akin to anticipation. His broad shoulders hunched for a moment, then he shook his head and laughed.

"It'd be just like old times, but I have to pass," the big man replied. "I promised a lady I'd bring you back in one piece."

"What lady?"

Colt continued to shake his head. "What lady? Like I said, you can be as dumb as a mud fence at times, Robert. *Your* lady."

"Maggie?"

"I told you to hang onto her, didn't I? But did you listen? No. You tossed her away like yesterday's newspaper," Colt said, his voice gruff and reproachful. "Lucky for you she's every bit as tough as I thought she was and refused to stay tossed."

Robert felt so confused he couldn't think straight. "I don't understand. What are you talking about?"

"While you were out here stargazing and contemplating your navel, or whatever it is you do in this field all alone, she was moving her tail and convincing me and James you could salvage this mess," he told him curtly. "That's what I'm talking about. That woman has a lot of faith in you, Robert, and so help me, if you disappoint her—"

"Wait a minute. What do you mean she convinced you I can salvage this mess? Chapman's got the formula and there's nothing I can do to stop them from going into production."

Colt sighed. "I can't stand here and lecture you all night. I have things to do, like talking to the other board members and maybe grab hold of a few more shares of Trescott stock," he told Robert impatiently.

"What? Why would you—"

"If you're half the man I think you are and even a third of the man Maggie makes you out to be," he continued briskly, "I've got to get busy figuring out how to spend all the money you're going to make for Trescott Labs."

"But—"

"But nothing! I've got work to do and so do you," Colt said, pushing Robert toward his car. "Get your rear end back to town. If I were you the first thing I'd do would be to make up with that terrific woman you stumbled on, and then I'd listen to what she has to say. If she can talk a raging bull like James Trescott out of charging headlong into you I'd say she deserves at least that much, Robert."

Colt laughed at the perplexed look on Robert's face as he got into his car and drove off. "Lord knows, that woman could probably organize a herd of wild buffalo, but I'm still not so sure she hasn't bitten off more than she can chew."

After having a serious argument with himself all the way back to town, Robert decided that Colt was right. If Maggie had somehow managed to persuade Trescott to back off, the least he could do was talk to her, listen to her explanation. He was fully prepared to disbelieve everything she said, but he would listen.

But where would she be? Since it appeared she was still working for him no matter what he had said earlier, he figured the workshop would be the most logical place to start. Sure enough, there were lights on in the warehouse that shouldn't be on, and her car was parked in front of the building.

Confused, scowling, not knowing whether he was angry or elated at finding her there, he took the stairs two at a time and burst into the office.

"Putting in a little overtime?" he asked, unable to keep the sarcasm from his voice when he saw her going through his files.

She was as lovely as ever, and try as he might he couldn't prevent his pulse from quickening at the sight of her. He didn't know what was going on, but he did know he would never be able to get Maggie out of his system.

"Just undoing some of the damage I did this afternoon," she replied calmly. "We're going to need all the organization we can get around here if you're going to beat Craig at his own game."

"Beat Craig . . ." His confusion was finally getting the better of him. "Has everybody gone mad? Colt tracks me down to tell me Trescott has decided not to sue, apparently because of something you convinced them I could do, even though there isn't a chance in the world I could stop Chapman now," Robert said heatedly as he paced back and forth in front of her waving his hands. "Then I find you here going through my files after I fired you and—"

"You didn't," Maggie objected, her expression still placid as she continued working.

Robert stopped pacing. "I didn't what?"

"Fire me. You told me to go away. Those are two entirely different things," she explained. "Had you fired me, my responsibility as your employee would have ended. But you didn't. In a fit of masculine pique, you told me to go away because you mistakenly thought I had betrayed you." She shrugged. "Everybody's entitled to make mistakes, even a pompous jerk like you."

Fists clenched at his sides, Robert glared at her and asked incredulously, "Excuse me?"

"Pompous jerk," she repeated. "Someone who flies off the handle for no apparent reason, taking his frustrations out on innocent bystanders."

"I had plenty of reason!" he yelled. "And how can you possibly call yourself an innocent bystander, Maggie? Did I or did I not hear you offering to sell my ideas to that swine, Craig Smith?"

"You did."

"Ha!"

Maggie stopped what she was doing and faced him squarely. "But as an inventor you should know better than anybody that things are not always what they appear to be," she told him, anger creeping into her voice for the first time. "You once told me you got where you are today by not taking things at face value, by seeing beyond appearances, looking for the true meaning behind the facts."

"Wait just a minute. I—"

"Evidently you forgot your own axioms," she continued, "because what I was really doing in that park with Craig was trying to help you by setting him up, using the phase-two formula as bait to draw him out in the open." Now it was Maggie's turn to pace angrily, and as she did so her voice got louder. "But I didn't forget those axioms. When you jumped all over me, refused to even give me a chance to explain, I realized you had taken leave of your senses and that whatever you told me to do I could chalk up to insanity on your part."

Robert's face turned red with outrage. "Insanity?"

"Insanity, eccentricity, whatever you want to call it," Maggie shot back. "That's another thing I've learned working for you: You don't always know what you're saying even if you sound like you do. What's more, sometimes you forget how smart you are."

"You—" He stopped and blinked. "What?"

"Smart. Intelligent. You don't always act like one, Robert, but you're a genius," she replied. "I knew that if I could figure out the only logical solution to our dilemma, you would figure it out, too, once you calmed down. Since I wasn't fired and you had gone off somewhere, I saw it as my responsibility to take over for you until you did."

With that she grabbed a brand-new workshop log from the desk and strode purposefully out of the room. Robert stood there for a moment, stunned, then dashed after her and followed her downstairs. When she got to the workshops she began stacking the files he had left laying around into tidy piles.

"What are you doing?" he asked, trying to get his befuddled mind functioning.

"Getting this place ready for you to start work," she replied tersely. She slammed the new log down in front of him. "Here. I've already copied the contents of the phase-two file into this and witnessed the work."

Robert frowned. "But phase two is months, maybe years from realization."

"I know that. But what you have on it had to be properly documented as a possibly patentable offshoot on the formula Chapman has," she explained, regaining some control over her temper. "In addition to which you'll need the information right there to prove that your next idea grew out of your research and diligent workmanship."

"What next idea?" he asked, quite bewildered by her efficiency.

She stopped straightening up and pointed a finger at him. "I went to James and assured him you could do this, Robert, so you damn well better get cracking!"

He cleared his throat uneasily. "What did you tell him I could do, Maggie?"

"Improve the phase-one formula, of course," she replied with a long-suffering sigh. "Make it work faster, better, find a way for the face-lifting, skin-tightening effects to linger for a longer period of time. The only way we have of beating Chapman is to come up with a better product—and come up with it fast so Trescott can introduce it at the same time."

Robert stared at her, but he wasn't really seeing her. "An improved version," he mumbled, his tone distant as he considered what she had said. "Faster, better, longer lasting."

Suddenly he opened the log and pulled a pen from his pocket, scribbling furiously as he followed some train of thought. Maggie watched, a small smile forming itself upon her face. Then she grinned and walked over to where he stood bent over the log as he wrote. She put her head close to his.

"I think I hear gears whirring," she said softly.

"Hmm?" Robert looked up, his mind slowly returning from its flight of creative fancy. "Excuse me?"

She kissed him on the cheek. "I knew you could do it once you put that brain of yours to work."

"I haven't done anything yet," he said doubtfully. "But thanks for the vote of confidence." He closed the notebook, then reached out and gently stroked her hair. "Why, Maggie? After all those things I said and the stupid way I acted. Why didn't you just leave me to fend for myself?"

"Because you hadn't fired me. Taking care of you is still my job, one I happen to like a great deal." Maggie put her arm around him, hugging him close. "And because I love you, you crazy nut. Didn't you know?"

Robert closed his eyes and sighed. "No. I hoped you did. That's why it hurt so much when I thought . . . but then, I've been told twice tonight I can be incredibly stupid at times." He turned and pulled her into his arms, covering her face with soft, sweet kisses. "I love you, Maggie. I can't imagine life without you. Thank God you didn't listen to me when I told you to go away. You were right. I was temporarily insane."

He felt so good against her, she couldn't get enough of the way his hands glided up and down her spine. Shivers of love and relief made her cling even tighter to him.

"Let's face it, my love," she whispered in his ear. "We're both brilliant. We work too well together to be separated by foolishness."

"I love you, Maggie. I love you so much."

Robert kissed her, his tongue delving into her

253

mouth, the taste of her sweeter to him than water to a man lost in the desert. He had been lost in a desert of his own making, but she had found him, saved him, and he vowed never to leave her again.

"Let's promise never to fight," he said.

Maggie chuckled. "Are you kidding?" she murmured against his demanding lips. "I'm sure we'll have plenty of fights before this is all over."

"I suppose you're right," he agreed with a wry grin. "We'll just have to promise always to try to see beyond the facts. I won't forget again that things aren't always what they seem."

"Neither will I." Maggie kissed him deeply, allowing her love for him to flow out of her to surround him. Then she pulled back slightly to look at his face, noticing he was frowning slightly. "What's wrong?"

He hugged her reassuringly. "Nothing, really. I have you and that's all that matters. But . . ."

"Tell me."

"I just hope I can live up to this promise you made for me, that's all."

Maggie stroked the worry lines from his brow with a soft touch from her hand. She wanted to console him, reassure him, and grinned mischievously as she decided on an enjoyable way to do so.

"You can do it, Robert. You're a brilliant man." She winked at him, taking his hand and leading him to the cozy studio apartment where they had shared such delicious ecstasy together. "Not to mention very sexy."

She released his hand to turn down the covers on the bed. Though he knew full well what she had in mind and wanted her just as much, something wouldn't let him settle down. Frowning, he paced around the room, suddenly very uneasy about the situation she'd gotten him into. He wished he had as much faith in himself as she did.

"What if I can't improve the formula?" he asked.

"Then we pick up the pieces and go from there." Maggie stopped his nervous pacing with her actions as she tossed her shirt to the floor. "But you'll find a way, I know you will. Right now, however," she added in a sultry voice, "I think you need something to relax you, take your mind off all your problems."

Robert's eyes widened as he watched the rest of her clothes fall to the ground. "Maggie . . ."

"Join me?" she invited, curling herself seductively on the bed. "No barriers allowed. I want nothing between us," she murmured as he started toward her.

Quickly, trying to forget his cares, he shed his clothes and slid down beside her. "I do need you," he whispered, gathering her in his arms and holding her close. The arousing, totally feminine scent of her body was setting him afire, and he allowed himself the distracting luxury of her touch. "I need you so much."

His body was wound up as tight as a loaded spring coil, ready to go bouncing off at a moment's notice. He couldn't think straight anymore. Everything hinged on his being able to come up with a better formula. What if he didn't? She had assured him she would stand by him no matter what, had certainly proved she was willing to, but still . . .

"Relax," Maggie ordered softly as she rolled him over and began massaging the tight muscles of his neck and shoulders. "Let your mind go blank, let it float free like an eagle, soaring through a cloudless blue sky without a care in the world."

Her soothing voice continued to caress him as her hands performed the same magic on his tight muscles, easing the tension from his mind and body. Like water washing away sand, her tenderness lapped at the unessential elements of worry and doubt, leaving only the barest needs behind.

He turned over on his back and began to stroke her smooth skin, rich velvet beneath his touch. She was such a giving person, willing to bestow upon him her greatest gift: herself. Her nimble, tantalizing fingers were growing bolder with each passing stroke. Robert looked at her face and felt his breath catch in his throat.

She wet her lips provocatively. "Like that?"

His eyes were glued to the shimmering wetness of her mouth. "Are you playing with me?" he asked as he watched the tip of her tongue slowly trace her full upper lip.

"Mmm, yes," she murmured sensuously. "Do you like it?"

"Too much." He moved over and trapped her legs beneath his. "You're playing with fire."

Maggie wiggled suggestively. "I like your fire," she whispered. "Come here and I'll put it out." Sliding her body on top of his, she moaned in pleasure. "Eventually," she promised, her voice husky with emotion.

His hand slid around her neck as he brought their lips closer, almost but not quite touching, until he could feel her warm breath on his face, caressing him. Her passion-filled eyes, hazel flecked with emerald-green, gazed back at him with sensual promise.

Time stood still until her tongue darted out to lick his lips, only to slip back into hiding. With his tongue he carefully traced the delicate lines of her mouth, coaxing her to open up to him. The rose-red bud of her lips flowered with a willing warmth, opening up to enclose him deep within her.

They were fused as one, reveling in their heat and desire for each other as they flew higher and higher, together trying to find that elusive star which would send them soaring and cover them in something more precious than gold dust. They found just such a star, holding each other tightly as it spun them aloft, their moist, feverish skin molding them together until reality slowly descended upon them once again.

"Thank you, Maggie," Robert whispered, his voice ragged with emotion.

"I love you, Robert."

"I love you too." He looked into her eyes. "Maggie, I . . ." The uncertainty of his future held him back. What did he have to offer her at this time other than undying love? He wanted to give her so much more, but what if he couldn't beat the odds?

Maggie seemed to understand. She held him close and assured him once again. "Shh. We'll beat this, Robert. And we'll do it together."

CHAPTER FIFTEEN

"More lanolin?"

"Possibly."

"Alcohol?"

Robert grimaced. "No. It tends to dry the skin and won't mix with the new ingredient anyway."

"Estrogen?" Maggie inquired.

"Absolutely not. Neither I nor Trescott approve of using hormones in cosmetics."

Maggie sighed and crossed it off the list of additives they were sorting through. She put down her clipboard and went to the coffeepot to pour them both another cup. Why did they call it burning the midnight oil? What they were really doing was burning caffeine.

"Sugar?" she asked.

Robert looked up from the log he was scribbling in and stared at her. "Sugar? Why on earth is that on a list of cosmetic additives?"

"I meant for your coffee," she explained, managing to laugh despite her exhaustion.

"Oh. Yes, please. I need energy."

Getting James Trescott's approval to use the rare, expensive ingredient in the face-lift cream had been easy compared to adding it to the formula. His fears about instability were proving correct, with the results starting out near perfect and turning into total disasters.

It wasn't that the additive didn't work; James's chemists had done enough testing to show that it was indeed the magic element Robert thought it was. The problem with the stuff was that it didn't seem to agree with one or more of the other ingredients. At first the mixture produced a lovely, skin-tingling cream, then it slowly hardened into a substance that wouldn't even come out of the test tube. They needed to find the correct balance, and thus far had succeeded only in making some spectacular messes.

"Well," Robert said around a sleepy yawn, "I guess we could always market this stuff as a world-class glue."

They toiled on, finally collapsing onto the bed in the studio apartment and falling asleep in each other's arms. It was a pattern they repeated over and over the next week, taking some consolation from the fact that Trescott's people were working around the clock as well.

Step by slow step Robert solved the problems which confronted him, while Maggie painstakingly recorded every nuance of his research and passed the results on to the equally meticulous chemists at Trescott Labs. At least her trips to see James got her out in the fresh air. Robert wasn't so lucky, and by the end of the second laborious week she was more than a little worried about him.

He had been secretive all day, ignoring James Trescott's phone calls and suddenly insisting on making his own log entries, leaving Maggie with little to do but pace the office and wonder what he was up to. Even the prospect of Inez's cooking couldn't interrupt him; she had dropped off some food for them again this afternoon and again he had refused to take time out for such trivial matters.

At wit's end, Maggie finally decided she would march right into his workshop, force-feed him and even knock him on the head to make him sleep if necessary. Making as much noise as possible, she clamored down the stairs and approached him, receiving little more than an impatient wave of his hand for her efforts.

"Robert?"

"Hmm?"

"Time to eat and get some rest."

"Hmm."

Maggie sighed in exasperation, then went to the tiny apartment kitchen to heat the food and set the table. When everything was ready she returned to the workshop and confronted him again.

"Robert?" He nodded but didn't look up from the papers spread out over his lab counters. She tried again, her voice louder and sharper this time. "Robert!"

What was the use? He was so engrossed in this project the place could probably blow up around him and he'd still be sitting there lost in thought. He didn't even blink when Maggie waved her hand in front of his face.

"Your Mercedes is on fire, Robert."

"Hmm."

"I'm leaving you to become a cheerleader for the Dallas Cowboys, Robert."

He mumbled again, and she decided he had fallen asleep with his eyes open. Very gently, Maggie squeezed his nose shut and placed her hand over his mouth.

"What the—"

"Welcome to the world of the living."

Robert gasped for breath. "Why did you do that?" he demanded indignantly. "Can't you see I'm concentrating?"

"It's time to eat."

"I'll eat later."

"You'll eat now!" she informed him. "And then you're going to get some sleep."

He didn't move, just stared at her, a blank look on his tired face. She peered into his eyes and threatened, "I'm going to start throwing your papers all over this room if you don't do as I say."

"You wouldn't."

"Try me," she invited, her hands hovering over the very papers he'd been working on.

He knew that look on her face by now. "All right. I'll eat, but I don't have time to sleep.

Where's the food?" he asked, giving in reluctantly. She was more than capable of carrying out her threat.

"This way," she murmured, leading him to the kitchen and the waiting food. He was almost out on his feet. "Sit down before you fall down."

Robert did as instructed, inhaling deeply. His eyes closed and he sighed. "If I'm dreaming, please don't wake me up just yet."

Maggie smiled at the relaxed expression crossing his face. She set a bowl of rice and green chili in front of him, then added the warm tortillas Inez had made that morning.

"Thank you, Maggie."

"You're welcome. Inez and I decided it was time to see if you were still alive. If you could resist this," she said, gesturing to their dinner, "then there wasn't any hope for you at all."

They ate in companionable silence, Maggie enjoying the transformation coming over him. First his color returned, then his eyes opened wider and took on their usual bright gleam. He even smiled.

Maggie smiled back. "You'll never live this one down," she teased as he took another helping.

"What?"

"Inez's food bringing you back to life. She'll claim you'll have to be her slave from now on."

He took her hand, pressing his lips to the sensitive skin of her palm. "She'll have to stand in line. First and foremost I'm a slave to your gentle touch."

"I was beginning to think you were a slave to your work," she returned dryly. "How's it coming?"

"You already know I found the problem additive and replaced it with an agreeable ingredient. James's chemists are almost done testing the formula under every imaginable circumstance, and—"

"Then what on earth are you doing?" Maggie interrupted.

Robert sighed, his expression distant. "I still think there could be even more dramatic changes with this cream, but I can't pinpoint exactly what's holding up the process."

"Trescott's satisfied?"

"Yes. I'm the one who isn't," he mumbled. "Maggie, there has got to be a way to help even the most damaged skin."

Maggie was more confused than ever. "What else is there? It has the startling effect of a face-lift if used daily."

"That's just it. You have to use it daily and continue to use it for the cream to work. I want it to be something you would use maybe a few times a year."

Maggie got out of her chair, debating whether to reassure him or knock some sense into him. She decided he was too tired to see what he was doing to himself. It had been her job to organize him into this, and now she had to organize him out.

She stood behind him, massaging his tight neck

muscles and speaking in a soothing voice. "Robert, you worked on this project for a long time to get the formula this far," she reminded him.

"Yes, but—"

"And maybe there are improvements you can make, but it will take still more time for you to find the solution. If you continue to work yourself to the point of exhaustion you may never find the answers you so desperately seek." Kissing him on top of the head to take the sting from her words, she added, "It's time to stop, my love."

Robert tilted his head back to look at her face, seeing the concern there. Then he looked off into space for a moment before nodding reluctantly. "You're right."

"Aren't I always?" she teased.

"Sassy too," he murmured as her hands worked their magic on his stiff neck. "Have I ever told you how lovely your fingers are?"

"Not lately, and that's another reason I want you to stop. I want you back." She blew softly in his ear. "I could do an even better job if you didn't have any clothes on."

"Are you propositioning me?"

"Are you accepting?"

"Yes," he whispered.

He stood up, using his hips to move her across the room. They tumbled together onto the bed, their lips touching with a mutual sigh of satisfaction.

"Are you sure you wouldn't rather sleep?"

"Later," he replied softly. "I've just made an important discovery. It seems success is a powerful aphrodisiac."

"So I see," Maggie murmured throatily. She stroked him, and his moan of pleasure was music to her ears. "I've just made an important discovery of my own."

CHAPTER SIXTEEN

Two weeks later, James, Robert, Maggie, and the ever-mysterious Colt sat in the spacious backseat of the Trescott company limousine, looking at the people crowded outside the department store. This was the first retail outlet to sell Trescott Phase One, and they were doing so much business the clerks couldn't keep up.

"Nice crowd," Colt said.

"Predominantly female, though," James noted with a worried frown. "I was hoping more men would want to buy some."

Maggie chuckled. "How do you know they're all buying it for themselves, James? I notice most of them are walking out with more than one bottle. Maybe the extras are for their husbands and boyfriends."

"Hmm," James murmured thoughtfully, smiling again. "You've got a point there, Maggie." He popped the cork on a bottle of champagne and poured them all a glass, then lifted his own in a toast. "To Robert, for working so hard and so brilliantly, and for forgiving me for being such a pain."

"And to Maggie," Colt added, "for standing by him through thick, thin, and several gloppy stages in between."

Maggie sipped the bubbling wine. "Like going home every night plastered with his experiments until he came up with the right combination," she commented dryly.

"It wasn't that bad," Robert objected.

"I suppose not." She touched her face. "My complexion has never been better."

Robert hugged her close. "Phase One didn't do that, dear. You've always been this beautiful."

They sat drinking champagne and watching the store rapidly sell out of the cream Robert's genius had created, James and Colt calculating profits while Maggie and Robert simply enjoyed the end of their hard work. It had been mind-numbing and exhausting labor, marked with tempestuous arguments just as Maggie had predicted, but the whole experience had only managed to bring them closer together.

Robert had had to draw upon every iota of her organizational talent to beat the clock and his less-capable former assistant. But they had done it, saved his reputation and ensured a place in cosmetic history for him and Trescott Labs. At the moment, however, the two lovers were much more interested in the prize they had found in each other, a love so strong it would outlast all their other achievements.

"Did anyone ever find out why Craig hated me so much?" Robert asked.

Colt shrugged. "According to James's spy, he was jealous of your success. Still maintains the idea was his and that he could invent rings around you if somebody would give him the opportunity."

"Fat chance," James said sarcastically. "Marsha Lane is using this fiasco as the final wedge to get rid of Dennis Chapman once and for all." He smiled. "And as for Craig and Dennis, well, I don't think their partnership ended on a happy note. Dennis claims he didn't have any idea the formula was stolen and is threatening to sue Craig."

Maggie grinned, relishing the thought. "Really?"

Colt nodded. "It won't come to anything, though. Craig has crawled back under whatever rock he came from and Dennis is going to be too busy trying to save even his figurehead status at Chapman Corporation," he told them. "Eventually they may come out with an inferior product, but for now we're home free. All we have to do is sit back and watch our stock soar."

"You're sure you don't want your picture on the Phase One label, Robert?" James asked, his tone serious though his eyes sparkled mischievously. "You could become a household hero if you wanted to."

Maggie cleared her throat. "He's sure."

"You mean you don't want all those women gazing fondly at Robert's face in their bedrooms every night?" Colt inquired, laughing so hard he almost spilled his wine.

"Does sound kind of intriguing, doesn't it?" Robert interjected thoughtfully.

She glared at them both. "I can see I'm going to have to organize it so you two don't get together often."

"I've decided to remain anonymous, James," Robert said solemnly.

"Wise choice."

James Trescott sighed, making a mental note to increase production by 25 percent since the results of this test marketing campaign appeared so successful. He looked at Robert, his expression turning thoughtful.

"So, Robert," he said casually, "when can we expect to see the Phase Two body cream?"

"Ha! The first thing I'm going to do is take a vacation, and then I think I'll steer clear of cosmetics for a while."

"At least until our maintenance crew can clean up the workshop from the mess he made on this stuff," Maggie agreed.

"That bad?" Colt wanted to know.

"Worse." She made a face. "We have white cream dripping from the ceilings."

Robert grinned. "I don't know. I think it's kind

of exciting, walking through the place and dodging the glops."

"I'll glop you," Maggie threatened.

"I thought you enjoyed cleaning up," he said, tweaking her nose gently and chuckling in his evil, roguish way.

Maggie thought of the long sensuous showers they had taken together after each disaster. "Some cleanups are better than others," she replied, fighting a blush.

"I'll say."

"Be that as it may," James continued, "we're still very interested in Phase Two."

Robert barely heard him. He was gazing into Maggie's eyes, knowing she had the same thing in mind as he did. "We'll discuss it later, James. Right now we have to be getting back to the workshop to take care of some, um, urgent matters. Don't you agree, Maggie?"

"I most heartily agree, Robert," she murmured. "We have to take care of these things as they arise."

Maggie swam the length of the pool and back, the glaring sun forming mesmerizing patterns on the blue water. Robert should have been back by now. When he had called he said they needed to talk but refused to tell her what it was they needed to talk about. She had agreed to wait for him here, but she was impatient to see him again, needing to

271

feel his reassurance, his strength against her softness.

Exhausted, she pulled herself out of the pool and blotted most of the water off with a fluffy towel. Her burnt orange and turquoise maillot molded to her body like a second skin. It was a gift from Robert, along with a minuscule black bikini she hadn't worked up the courage to wear yet.

"Blast these new inventions," she grumbled, struggling with the top on a container of suntan lotion. "I will not admit defeat to a twist cap." Finally the obstinate bottle yielded to her fiddling and she started to smooth the lotion on her golden skin, debating with herself over whether to change suits. At last she decided she should. "I guess I am supposed to give this stuff a thorough test."

There wasn't enough material on either piece of the black bikini to adequately cover her, but it would be perfect for tanning—and for tantalizing Robert when he finally arrived. He had sounded so worried when he called. What could be so important?

Sprawled out on the comfortable pool-side chaise, she struggled to stay awake, but was lulled by the blazing sun into dreamland. She dozed until her small timer buzzed to let her know it was time to turn over. A raging red sunburn was the very last thing she wanted to cope with. After spreading lotion on as much bare skin as she could reach between the tiny black scraps of her suit, she got up and reset the timer, then settled back down again on her stomach.

Unbeknown to Maggie, Robert had been watching, feeling like a voyeur in his own home. She filled the black bikini well, better then his vivid imagination had ever dreamed. He quickly stripped off his clothes and pulled on a pair of brief maroon swim trunks.

His footsteps were silent on the red tile. She couldn't see his approach from the house; her head was buried in her arms. He squeezed a generous amount of lotion on his palm and rubbed it between his hands to warm it.

"Hello," he whispered, right before he placed his hands on her back. "I've come to help."

"Robert!" She looked at him over her shoulder and started to get up. "You certainly took your time. What's so important—"

"Shh. Keep still and relax," he murmured, pressing her back down on the cushioned chaise. "You've missed a few spots here and there." His hands glided over her back, touching every nook and cranny with deliberate, sensual stokes. "Isn't that better?"

"Mmm, lovely," she whispered, resting her cheek against the cushions. "Absolute heaven."

"I couldn't agree more." He smoothed lotion over and around her dangling arms. The taut skin on her thighs beckoned for his touch and he obliged. With whisper soft caresses he glided his hands over the womanly lines and curves of her

273

body, memorizing each detail beneath his finger-tips.

"Time's up," he murmured as the buzzer went off. A rogue finger slid down her spine and over the bare skin of her buttocks, his mind spinning at her soft moan of pleasure. "Let's swim and cool us both off."

Maggie rolled over and watched as he executed a perfect shallow dive into the pool, then eased her body into the clear blue water. Until he was ready to talk to her she was going to have to display an enormous amount of patience.

All Robert really wanted to do was sweep her up in his arms and take her to his bed, then slowly peel the tiny scraps of cloth from her body. But they had to talk things out first. He wanted the decisions facing them to be made rationally, calmly, not as the result of some heated aftermath of blazing passion.

Maggie headed for the edge of the pool and pulled herself out of the water. Much more swimming today and she'd be ready for the prune hall of fame. She crossed her ankles and hugged her legs with her arms, her chin resting on her knees, waiting for Robert to finish. He certainly had a lot of energy today; she could think of a much better way to use it than doing laps. But he obviously had a lot on his mind.

Robert swam some more laps after she left the pool. No time like the present, he thought as he heaved his body out beside her. He was as cooled off as he was ever going to get around her.

"We have to talk," he announced, trying to gauge her mood by looking into her exquisite hazel eyes.

They expressed so much of her feelings, changing with each emotion she felt. The flecks of green in their depths seemed to grow larger with passion, smaller with anger. At the moment she seemed curious, a bit impatient, the best he could hope for under the circumstances.

"I'm all ears," Maggie replied. She watched as he stood up and dried himself off. "Inside?" she asked, slipping on the white cotton robe he held open for her.

He nodded, his expression so troubled she started frowning herself. She followed him into the living room, her eyebrows arching when he offered her a drink. Brandy in the afternoon? she thought. This must be serious.

"Well?" she demanded when he handed her a snifter of the golden liquid. "What is so dire that you figure I'll need this to brace me?"

"Maggie . . ." He paused, then turned from looking out the living room window to face her squarely. "How do you feel about children?"

The glass started to slip from her hand as the content of his question registered. She gripped it more firmly, glad to have something to hold onto as she looked into his gray eyes. It was a simple question, but she had the feeling a great deal hinged on her answer.

"Why?" she asked.

He ignored the perplexed look on her face. "Do you want to have any?"

"Well, I've always thought I would. Someday." She cocked her head to one side and continued to gaze at him in puzzlement. "Why?" she asked again.

Robert started prowling around the room, unable to sit still as he spoke. "Two men I know got divorced recently because of different opinions with their wives over that," he replied. "That's why."

Divorce? They hadn't even discussed marriage and he was talking about divorce. "Because of what?"

"Children," he bit out, pacing the length of the room.

"Robert! Stop pacing and start talking," she ordered, her patience gone. "I'm completely in the dark about this."

Did he really want to marry such a bossy woman? He sat down in the chair beside the couch and looked at her. Yes, he most definitely did. He couldn't imagine life without Maggie now. She was also sexy, beautiful, fun, efficient. . . .

"Robert," she prompted softly. "Divorce?"

"Oh, yes," he murmured, coming back to the present. "Two men I know recently dissolved their relationships because of children." He reached out and brushed her furrowed brow with his fingertips, easing the delicate skin back to smoothness. "For different reasons: One wanted them and one didn't and they were with the wrong mates."

Maggie held her breath. "And?"

"I wanted to know how you felt," he whispered, the tips of his fingers caressing her cheek. Still restless, he got up and slid onto the couch beside her, taking her face between his hands. "Before I asked you."

She breathed very softly. "Asked me what?"

"Will you marry me?"

"Yes!"

His black brows arched in surprise at her quick reply. "Don't you want to think about this?"

Maggie kissed him and laughed out loud. "I already have," she assured him. "But I thought you'd never get around to asking." She sighed dramatically and added, "You had just two more days. It's so much better this way, though."

"What way?"

She jumped up, dancing around the room in unrestrained joy. "Just think, now I won't have to tell our children I proposed to you."

"And what, pray tell, would be so terrible about that?"

"You wouldn't want them to think I was fast, would you?" she asked indignantly. "Or that you were slow?"

"I'll show you fast." He got up and caught her

as she twirled around the room. "Seriously, though, aren't you worried about our differences?"

Maggie shook her head emphatically. "Not one bit. They'll make life much more interesting," she murmured as she removed first his robe, then her own. "For instance, I see some very nice differences right now," she added in a provocative whisper, resting her hands on his hips and gently kneading his bare skin. Slowly, sensuously, she removed his brief maroon swimsuit. "Give you any ideas?"

"Many," he whispered, running his hands over her body as he stripped her tiny bikini off. "Enough for a lifetime."

"I want you," she moaned, his teasing hands igniting the smoldering desire coursing through her body. "Now."

Robert was more than ready to oblige. His strength as solid as a pillar of stone, he lifted her, holding her tightly against him as they came together in fiery passion, her legs wrapping around him in an effort to control their ecstasy. The flames of desire consumed them so swiftly they soared to the pinnacle at a shattering speed. Breathless, shaken, they collapsed in a tangle and held each other close, their tongues dueling as they reveled in the sweet afterglow.

Somewhere in the house a door slammed, startling them back to reality. "What rotten timing," Robert grumbled.

"Oh, I don't know," Maggie said with a contented sigh. "A moment sooner . . ."

"Robert, the groceries are waiting," Inez called from the kitchen.

"Damn!"

They flew apart and scrambled around on the living room floor for their suits and robes, fumbling as they tried to dress quickly. Maggie laughed at the look of annoyance on his face, then kissed him until he smiled again.

Inez looked over her shoulder as they entered the kitchen. "Hello, Maggie." She grinned. To Maggie it seemed a particularly knowing smile. "How are you?"

"I'm fantastic," she replied, laughing when Inez's grin grew even broader.

Robert ignored them and headed out to the garage. He'd forgotten all about the grocery shopping trip. The quicker he brought everything in, the quicker Inez would leave so he could get back to what he wanted to be doing.

"Any luck?" Inez asked after he left for the third time to get the groceries.

Maggie walked over and hugged the older woman. "Yes!"

"When's the wedding?"

"We didn't get that far, Inez. He just proposed," she answered, unpacking one of the grocery sacks.

A look of distress crossed the housekeeper's face. "Oh, no!" she cried in dismay. "I interrupted things."

Maggie rushed to reassure her. "No, you didn't. I—"

"Yes, she did," Robert cut in, setting the last of the sacks down on the counter.

"Robert!"

"Maggie!" he mimicked.

Inez wasn't the slightest put out by his gruff accusation. "Where's her ring?" she wanted to know.

"How do you know I bought a ring?"

Inez put her hands on her hips and glared right back at him. "I know you, Robert Langley. You like your mark of ownership on everything that belongs to you."

"Maggie's not a thing!"

"No, she's a very lovely person, who for some crazy reason has decided to marry the likes of you." She rolled her eyes expressively at him in disbelief.

"I'll have you know I'm a very lovable person!" he objected heatedly.

"Ha!"

Maggie sat down at the kitchen table, enjoying their debate. It was her fondest wish that Inez stay with them. She would need all the help she could get to keep track of Robert. Though she knew the pair looked upon arguing as a kind of enjoyable sport, when their voices got to a certain level she decided it was time for her to enter the conversation.

"Well, Robert?" she asked. "Did you buy a ring?"

He stopped and looked at her. "Yes."

"Where is it?"

"I . . ." There was no way around this. "I'm not sure."

Inez laughed loudly. Maggie joined her. "At least he's honest, Inez. It's one of his most lovable qualities."

"See? I told you I was lovable."

"She's just humoring you," Inez returned. "You'd better get that ring on her finger before she comes to her senses."

"Did you take it out of the car?" Maggie asked.

His face reddening, Robert turned on his heel and walked back out to the garage, grumbling all the way. Sure enough, the ring he'd bought was still in his car.

"At least I remembered to buy it," he muttered when he returned to the kitchen.

"Give it to her before you lose it again," Inez told him as she finished putting away the groceries.

He walked over to Maggie and slid the ring on her finger. "We'll pick out our wedding bands together. I wanted you to have this as your engagement ring."

Tears shimmered in her eyes at his thoughtfulness. It was a ring from an antique shop they had visited together, one she had instantly fallen in love with—just like him. But the intricately strung gold was now wrapped around a pear-shaped diamond instead of the original cut glass.

"Oh, Robert! It's my ring! Thank you!" she

281

whispered, kissing him softly, his face cradled in her hands.

"See you tomorrow," Inez announced, picking up her purse. "I'll have to keep visiting other babies until you have some of your own." She looked at the happy couple, her eyes twinkling. "You do know how that works?"

"Good-bye, Inez," they intoned together as she waltzed out the door.

"Alone at last," Robert murmured, pulling Maggie tightly into his arms. "Where were we?"

"Don't tell me you've forgotten your place?" she teased.

Robert kissed her. "No. I think I have this design all figured out," he replied as he picked her up and carried her into his bedroom.

"Design?"

"Love's design, sweet Maggie." What a prize she was. Beauty, intelligence, loyalty, and strength, the only woman in the world for him. "It's a plan I want to follow with you forever."

Maggie covered his face with tiny kisses. "Are you sure you can manage to keep us on track?"

"I think I can manage this part," he assured her, reclining beside her on the bed. His lips traced patterns on her heated skin, then he looked into her hazel eyes, his gaze hungry.

"Mmm. So can I. All it takes is a little organization."

"Go ahead. Organize me."

"I will, my love," she promised. "Always."